THE APOTHECARY'S DAUGHTER

Keziah Sephton is kept busy caring for three generations of her family, as well as running the family apothecary shop. George Cunliffe has loved Keziah since they were youngsters, and when Benedict Clay arrives at the shop claiming to be blood kin, and is welcomed into the heart of the family, George is immediately suspicious of the soft-spoken Southern gentleman's motives ... After her grandmother's precious Book of Hours disappears, Keziah is tormented by treacherous doubts and swiftly enmeshed in a shocking spiral of deception, betrayal, ruthless ambition — and cold-blooded murder.

JUNE DAVIES

THE APOTHECARY'S DAUGHTER

Complete and Unabridged

LINFORD
Leicester

First published in Great Britain in 2013

First Linford Edition
published 2014

A catalogue record for this book is available
from the British Library.

ISBN 978–1–4448–2006–5

Published by
F. A. Thorpe (Publishing)
Anstey, Leicestershire

Set by Words & Graphics Ltd.
Anstey, Leicestershire
Printed and bound in Great Britain by
T. J. International Ltd., Padstow, Cornwall

This book is printed on acid-free paper

1

Dusk was falling as Keziah Sephton moved about her father's apothecary, turning up the whale-oil lamps just a touch more before fetching the wooden steps and clambering up to dust the shelf of bottles, flasks, phials, pots and jars. She'd no sooner started than the polished brass bell above the shop door jingled and, twisting around atop the shelf-ladder, Keziah glanced down over her shoulder.

'Oh,' she sighed, her forehead creasing into a frown as she caught hold of her black skirts with one hand and descended the ladder's worn-smooth steps. 'It's you, George.'

The sturdy, broad-shouldered young man strode inside, bringing with him a blast of keen air. He removed his cap and grinned across at her. 'I've had better welcomes, Keziah Sephton! I can go out and come back in again, if tha likes!'

Despite her concerns, Keziah's pale face broke into a ready smile. 'I'm sorry, George! I didn't mean it the way it sounded. Pa was called back to the almshouse first thing this morning and that brass bell's never stopped ringing since! The shop's been so busy I haven't had a chance to do any chores in the house. I've had to leave Gran on her own preparing supper, Edith'll be waiting for me outside the rectory as soon as her lessons finish — '

'And you've been left on your own to cope with everything?' he chipped in with a resigned sigh. 'Hardly anything new about *that*, is there?'

'It's not Pa's fault,' Keziah returned defensively. 'With more and more folk falling ill down at Quarry End and in the almshouse, he's sorely needed there!'

'Ey, steady on!' George protested mildly, holding up a calloused hand. 'I'm not saying owt against your pa. It's only him and his remedies that's easing the suffering of them poor souls living at the old workings. There's bad air and foul water down at the quarry, always has been. Small wonder fever's come to them again and spread into the almshouse.'

'I'm sorry, George.' She smiled ruefully. 'I didn't mean to snap your head off!'

'You're put upon, Kez. Have been for a long while. Your pa's made Samuel an equal partner now, so why isn't that clever brother of yours here in the apothecary pulling his weight?' demanded George scathingly. 'You do far more than your share of the work, and fair's fair — though it's obvious Samuel cares nowt for fairness and takes advantage of your good nature every chance he gets!'

'He had an appointment today,' she murmured by way of excusing her brother's absence. Inwardly, however, Keziah had to agree with every word George said. Since completing his education at York and returning home, Samuel had shown no interest whatsoever in the apothecary their father had spent a lifetime establishing. 'He'd arranged to visit old school friends up at Castlehill.'

'The Baldwins, no doubt,' commented George scornfully, taking a case of liniment and moving behind the wide oak counter. 'Here, stand clear and let me stack these bottles for you. Up on t'top shelf do they go?'

'Over to the left, next to the camphor oil.' She nodded, critically surveying the rows of shelves lining the apothecary's walls. 'We're running low on coltsfoot syrup and calendula salve, too. I must put a note in the ledger for Pa to make up fresh batches.'

'Kez, it's all very nice your Samuel having fancy notions about being a gentleman and hobnobbing with the gentry, but he's been handed a sound little business here,' went on George, glancing down to Keziah as he rowed the heavy brown glass bottles neatly into place. 'That lad doesn't know he's born! Why, if I had half his chances, I'd grab 'em with both hands!'

'Sammy's still young,' Keziah said loyally. 'I'm sure he'll settle down. It's just taking him a little while — to — to — '

'See sense and realise which side his bread's buttered?' prompted George, clumping down the shelf-steps and replacing them in the corner next to the dispensary. 'I were ten years old when Stanley Erskine took me on, fetching and carrying and loading up the waggons. I worked hard. Bit by bit, I learned the trade and earned Erskine's respect and now I all but run that business.

'Don't matter how hard I work though, nor how much the old man depends on me,' he went on resentfully. 'I'll never be anything more than a hired hand at Erskine's!'

'You're far more than that!' protested Keziah indignantly. 'Mr Erskine trusts you and relies upon you completely!'

'That's as may be. But some day soon Erskine's going to pack it in and sell up and I'll be out on my ear,' finished George bitterly, raking a hand through his thatch of sandy hair. 'Whereas that little brother of yours is set for life and couldn't care a toss — Ah, away! I've no place ranting at you, Kez! It's not for me to speak out anyhow.'

'If you cannot, then who can?' She reached out to gently squeeze his coarse hand and smiled up at him. 'You're a dear friend to this family, George! Besides, I fear your opinion of Sammy is nothing short of truth. I prefer to think him merely youthful and thought-less, but as yet Samuel has shown absolutely no regard for his family or his responsibilities here at the shop.'

George shrugged, his annoyance and frustration abating as he held both Keziah's hands in his own and gazed down into her clear grey eyes. 'I know nowt about grand folk, Kez. For all I know, Samuel might be every bit as fine

6

as them he rubs shoulders with at Castlehill. I only know it pains me seeing you run ragged every hour God sends while his lordship swans about enjoying himself!'

Keziah drew breath to respond but George pressed on earnestly.

'You've been that busy lately, you and me haven't had any time together at all!' he said, adding wryly, 'The only reason I've turned regular church-goer, is because at least I'm sure of seeing you at St Harmon's every Sunday — I don't go for Reverend Kennard's miserable sermons, that's for sure!'

'That's a shameful thing to say! Mr Kennard's a devout man and I'm sure he does his best when preaching,' scolded Keziah, not quite suppressing a smile. 'However, it *does* indeed seem one thing after another has gone wrong recently! First, Granny had her fall — and I'm ashamed to say I'd never realised how very hard Gran worked in this house, nor how much she did for us all, until she was laid-up and couldn't do it anymore. Then Edith was poorly for weeks. And since fever broke out at Quarry End, Pa's been down there day and night whenever he's needed . . . '

'I still don't understand why you're dead-set against getting a girl in to help out around the house!' grumbled George in exasperation. 'You should've done it years ago. A young lass wouldn't cost much, and happen she'd be only too glad to get board and lodging!'

'I've explained time and again, George, money isn't the point! Ma always put great love and pride into caring for her family and her home *herself*, and I'm more than happy to continue her ways,' replied Keziah resolutely, going on less severely. 'Besides, now Edith's recovered and back at school, Granny's on the mend and Sammy's home for good, I should be able to get out and about more often.'

'Amen to that! How is your gran, by the way? Last time I saw her she was still looking pretty frail. Has she picked up any?'

'She's much improved these past few days, thank goodness. Still housebound, of course, but now she's strong enough to get about the house with her stick she's a lot brighter. Granny's always liked keeping busy,' replied Keziah, adding soberly, 'Although in truth, she's not been herself since the fall last winter. Pa reckons the shock of falling and being badly hurt will take far longer to heal than the actual damage to her leg.'

'Makes sense. A scare like that is bound to take its toll on such an elderly lady,' agreed George practically. 'Once the weather is milder, we must get hold of one of them chairs on wheels — I'll look out for one when I'm travelling for Erskine's — Then at least we'll be able to take her to church and to visit that old friend of hers who lives by the river.'

'Miss Cranidge. Oh, yes, George — That's a splendid idea!' Keziah's face lit up. 'Gran would love to be able to attend church again. She has her little Book of Hours, of course. And Reverend Kennard visits regularly to pray with her, but Gran says it's not the same as actually going to worship at St Harmon's.'

'Saints preserve us! If I was poorly, a visit from Cyril Kennard would set me back months. I've yet to meet a more woebegone old beggar.'

'That's hardly fair!' remonstrated Keziah, barely keeping a straight face. 'Mr Kennard is, well, *serious*, that's all. Solemn. As befits his station. Remember, he sees a great deal of hardship and suffering amongst his parishioners here in Barrowby.'

'So does your pa, but he doesn't go round moaning and complaining the whole time. Anyhow, it was about St Harmon's I came in to see you, Kez. I wanted to ask if you're coming to the church social? There'll be dancing and musicians — Maybe Samuel will honour us common folk by giving us a tune on his fiddle!' He grinned, adding hopefully, 'What do you say, Kez? *Will* you come?'

'It sounds grand! I'd love to go,' she responded, her face wreathed in smiles. 'Providing Pa can be at home to look after Edith and sit with Granny. I really don't like leaving her alone in the house now. She knocked over her candle the other day and couldn't reach it. If Edith hadn't seen and snuffed it out, the parlour tablecloth would've gone up.'

George expelled a resigned sigh. He'd loved Keziah Sephton for as long as he could remember, and her devotion to her family was one of the many reasons he did so . . . But there was no denying Kez's devotion got in the way of their being sweethearts!

'We'll see then.' From his waistcoat pocket, George withdrew the worn timepiece he'd saved hard to purchase from the pawnbroker's on Castle Street and glanced at its plain face. 'Listen, I'll not be missed if I'm a bit longer getting back to the yard. Suppose I go up to the rectory and collect Edith from her lessons? I've got the waggon, so we'll not be but a short while.'

'Would you?' exclaimed Keziah, relieved. Edith and five other children were schooled by Mrs Kennard at the rectory on the edge of Castlehill. It was more than an hour's walk there and back, and Keziah had worried about Granny Meggan being on her own for such a time. 'It'd be a great help, and will save me closing up and leaving Gran!'

'That's settled then.' George bent and quickly kissed her cheek before replacing his cap at a jaunty angle. 'I'm on my way!'

'I'll have the kettle boiled when you get back!' she called after him as the brass bell jingled again and the shop door opened onto the dismal March afternoon. 'Some parkin hot from the oven too!'

'I'll drive all the faster, then!' returned George, raising a hand in cheery farewell.

Keziah slipped through the arch and along the hallway from the shop to glance in at the parlour. Meggan Worsley was seated in her chimney corner, needlework resting upon her lap and her head leaning against the wing of the high-backed chair as she dozed. Keziah had no sooner gently withdrawn the darning needle from between her grandmother's gnarled fingers and tucked the rug more snugly about her knees when the apothecary's brass bell rang impatiently.

Hurrying back into the shop, Keziah found one of Elijah Sephton's regular customers browsing the selection of cosmetic creams, lotions and soaps displayed along the side counter.

'Good afternoon, Mrs Sharples!' greeted Keziah politely. 'What can I do for you?'

'I want a tablet of that nice soap you got in at Christmas. The dear stuff that smells of flowers. It's a birthday present for my sister-in-law in Leeds and she's a fussy madam. Nothing but the best for her, and hang the cost! I need a pen'orth of wintergreen, a box of liver pills for Eric and another batch of my headache powders.'

'I'm afraid Pa's not back yet,' Keziah explained, cutting and weighing a tablet of smooth lavender-scented soap from an oblong wedge and wrapping it carefully in thickly waxed paper. 'He's at the almshouse.'

'Eric saw him heading out towards Quarry End before it were even daylight!' remarked Freda Sharples grimly. 'I hear the fever they've got down there in the workings is the worst in years. We'll be lucky if it doesn't spread up into the town and kill us all!'

'Pa and the others are doing everything possible to make sure that doesn't happen, Mrs Sharples.'

'He's nothing short of a saint, that father of yours! It's a thankless task, Lord knows,' observed Mrs Sharples morosely. 'To be sure, there's not many folk who'd bother tending the ills of paupers who don't have the brass to pay!'

'Pa does what he can.' Keziah's brow knitted, keenly aware how hard her father had been working since this latest outbreak of fever. 'The folk at the almshouse and those living in the quarry have nothing, and no kin to care about them.'

'True enough,' nodded Mrs Sharples, settling her ample frame into the chair beside the counter provided for the comfort of customers. 'Eric says lots of them in the almshouse are old soldiers and sailors. Men who've offered up their lives for their country and come home from war to end up beggars depending on charity for a crust and a bed. It's nothing short of a scandal!'

'When Pa returns,' went on Keziah, gathering Mrs Sharples's purchases from the shelves and the banks of small square drawers lining the shop's walls, 'I'll tell him you need more headache powders and as soon as he's made them up, I'll bring them round to you.'

'There's no call for such fuss, Keziah!' tutted Freda impatiently. 'You mind as good as your father does what goes into my powders — Why, more often than not, it's you as makes 'em up for me!'

'Yes, but Pa is here to supervise, Mrs Sharples,' explained Keziah politely, placing the soap and other packages into Freda's basket. 'It wouldn't be proper for me to dispense medicines on my own.'

'Away, lass! You've been helping your pa behind that counter since your face barely showed above it! You must know as much about remedies as him by now. You make them for me now so I can start taking 'em,' insisted Mrs Sharples. 'My head's thumping like a hammer in a forge. Besides, you don't even know when your father'll get back from Quarry End, and I can't be doing with waiting. Not with my head.'

'Very well. If you're sure,' conceded Keziah, moving beyond the oak partition with its small glass panes into the dispensary tucked at the rear corner of the shop. She consulted the record book of preparations Elijah Sephton kept locked in the desk drawer. 'Was the last mixture alright for you? Pa added extra feverfew and a touch of ginger to soothe the nausea you'd complained of.'

'Most efficacious,' replied Freda, shifting her weight on the chair and idly watching Keziah as she bustled about the dispensary selecting ingredients from the array of jars and bottles, taking the heavy marble pestle and mortar across to the work table, setting out the scales.

'You know, I reckon that fancy sign your father's had painted up above the shop now Samuel's home from York should read Elijah Sephton and *daughter* instead of *son*! You've helped out here since long before your poor mother passed away,' ruminated Freda Sharples while Keziah worked. 'I doubt I've seen Samuel behind this counter more times than I could count on one hand! He's a grand lad, mind. Smart as new paint. But if you ask me, Samuel's become too much the young gentleman to don an apron and spend the rest of his life serving behind the apothecary counter!'

'Samuel is young yet,' returned Keziah crisply, very carefully weighing ground root and blending it into the headache remedy. 'However now he's finished his education, he'll be able to take his place beside Pa. The apothecary is Samuel's birthright. Pa's worked extremely hard all his life so he can pass something worthwhile onto his only son.'

'Oftentimes sons don't want what their fathers want for them. They have bigger ideas for themselves,' opined Freda gloomily. 'Letting him take up that scholarship and go to York might've been a mistake — I told your mam as much at the time.

'Being in York and mixing with quality has opened the lad's eyes to a far grander world than Barrowby! He

18

certainly cuts a fine dash around town, mind,' she went on with a sniff. 'My Betsy's never done mooning over him! I said to her, Samuel Sephton's come home a gentleman with a prosperous future. He'll not look twice at a house maid like you, my girl!'

'Betsy and Sammy have been friends since they were Edith's age,' retorted Keziah coldly, glancing around the partition at the older woman. 'I'm sure that won't change a jot now they're grown.'

'Time'll tell,' commented Freda sceptically. 'Anyhow, I reckon Betsy had something more than friendship in mind! Can't say as I blame the lass. Samuel's the sort who can easy turn a young girl's head. I saw him t'other night coming out from the Rose and Crown with the Baldwin brothers and Reggie Crane. Dressed to the nines they were, and in high old spirits roaring off in a carriage up towards Castlehill.'

'Samuel knows the Baldwin brothers

from school. They were in a quartet together at York,' answered Keziah stiffly. Freda Sharples was a busybody and notorious gossip, and Keziah wanted to nip in the bud any talk of Sammy drinking and carousing around town with the Baldwin brothers, who were fast gaining a reputation in Barrowby for belonging to a wild and reckless set. 'General and Mrs Baldwin kindly invited Samuel to a musical evening at their home.'

'Very nice, I'm sure. Samuel still doing his music, is he? I recall as a bairn in church he always had a knack for it.' She hauled herself up from the chair and gathering her purchases, offered the coins to Keziah. 'Was that George Cunliffe I spotted earlier, swaggering out the shop looking pleased as punch with himself?'

Keziah nodded, her face lowered as she counted Mrs Sharples's change. 'George offered to collect Edith from the rectory, since I was busy here.'

Freda nodded sagely. 'He's a good

lad, is George Cunliffe. When are the pair of you going to name the day?'

Keziah gasped, her jaw dropping a little as colour crept into her pale cheeks. 'George and I are — are — '

'Don't you let him get away, Keziah! Dependable, solid husbands are hard to find,' cut in Freda briskly. 'I mean this only kindly and for your own good, but you're not getting any younger, are you? If you're not careful, the years will have slipped away and so will George and you'll be left standing behind that counter and looking after your father's household!'

With that, Mrs Sharples bustled from the apothecary into the gathering darkness.

Cleaning and tidying away the utensils she'd used in the dispensary, Keziah knew it was foolish to allow Freda Sharples to disconcert her — Why, everyone knew Freda could never resist meddling in other folks' affairs! — Nonetheless, the older woman's forthright comments irked her, and Keziah could not help but dwell upon them.

It was true she and George had known each other for years. They got along very well and were truly the greatest of friends. Keziah could not imagine life without him, but *marriage* . . . That had never been spoken of. Besides, George knew fine well Keziah couldn't possibly abandon her responsibilities and leave her father's house.

In the future, perhaps, when Granny Meggan was fully restored to health, and Samuel had properly taken his place in the apothecary and Edith was a little older . . . Perhaps *then* Keziah might be free to contemplate matrimony!

★　★　★

Meticulously entering details of the powders she'd prepared for Mrs Sharples into the medicine book, Keziah replaced the ledger into the desk drawer and took the opportunity of a quiet moment to go from the shop through to the parlour. It was a comfortable, warmly lit room that over the years had become her grandmother's very own corner of the tall, narrow house behind the apothecary. Meggan Worsley was seated at the fireside with her patchwork. She raised her face in the flickering light, the faded blue eyes shining when she smiled up at her eldest granddaughter.

'Hello, lass! Still no sign of our Sammy? Eee, but it's been another long day for you. That brass bell's never stopped ringing!'

'I may wrap it up in one of Pa's woolly nightcaps so I can't hear the wretched thing,' grinned Keziah, flexing the ache from her back and shoulders as she bent to stir the coals of the glowing fire. 'Do you need anything, Gran?'

'Nay, lass — I'm fine,' replied Meggan softly, turning stiffly in her chair to point through to the back kitchen. 'There's chocolate keeping hot in the jug and I buttered some oatcakes when you've time for a bite. I've not long looked at the parkin; it needs a while more to brown.'

'Thanks, Granny, but you really shouldn't have done all that baking!' protested Keziah, stooping to give Meggan's thin shoulders a quick hug before going through to pour the fragrant, steaming hot chocolate. 'You're supposed to be resting and keeping off your feet!'

'Wisht, I can get around gradually with my stick now, and I'd rather be doing something than just sat taking root!'

' . . . Ooh, this is nice!' murmured Keziah, warming her cold hands around the mug of chocolate as she returned to the parlour and perched on the edge of a chair close to the fire. 'I've put the kettle to boil. George has gone to the rectory for Edith, and I promised him tea and parkin when he gets back.'

'He's a good lad, and he thinks the world of you,' smiled Meggan, adding with an anxious frown, 'Your pa won't have had owt to eat or drink this whole day, Kezzie! He hadn't even eaten his breakfast when the messenger came for him and he rushed straight to the almshouse! I don't think he's letting on just how bad it is down there — Elijah's never been one to make a fuss.'

'He doesn't want us to worry,' sighed Keziah simply. 'I hope Pa'll be back soon though. He needs rest, Gran. He's worn out.'

Meggan nodded, and the two women sat with their thoughts in the firelight, silent save for the shifting of the coals and kindling in the grate before them.

'I'd best get back into the shop and sweep the floor ready for scrubbing,' Keziah said at last, rising reluctantly from the fireside. 'There's been a fair lot of mud and dirt trodden across it this day! Would you like me to bring the candle over so you can read, Gran?'

'No, thank you.' Meggan smiled up at her. 'I'd like my keepsake box, if you'll pass it down to me? I don't need a light to see my memories!'

Keziah reached up to the shelf in the chimney corner alcove and got down the well-worn, polished rosewood chest inlaid with mother-of-pearl that Granny had had since she was a girl. It contained all sorts of cherished possessions: old buttons, wisps of lace from Meggan's wedding bonnet and cuffs, love letters bound in ribbon from her husband, letters and cards from family and friends now long gone, a dog-eared and time-worn little book of prayers, two poorly drawn pencil sketches of the cottage on the sand-shore in Lancashire where generations of Meggan's family had been born and bred; babies' ribbons, posies of dried flowers, a curious pebble that sparkled like rainbows in sunlight, several playbills from the Harrogate Theatre and some sheets of the music she and Frank had enjoyed dancing to . . . Each keepsake holding a dear memory and telling a story Meggan Worsley recalled as though it had occurred only yesterday.

Keziah stood beside her grandmother a moment longer, watching Meggan's bony fingers gently smoothing the fragile pages of the tiny Book of Hours, its colourful illuminations still surprisingly vivid and bright. It had been passed down from mother to eldest daughter for many generations of Meggan's family and the tattered little book of prayers and psalms was very dear to the elderly woman; not least because of the solemn promise she'd made her own daughter when she'd lain desperately ill after Edith's birth.

'Your ma gave me the Book of Hours to keep safe for you, Kezzie,' remarked Meggan wistfully, glancing up at her granddaughter. 'I'm to pass it on to you when you come of age, as *she* would have done, had she still been with us — '

The ringing of the shop bell interrupted her words and Keziah reluctantly hurried from the parlour, leaving Meggan alone with her memories and precious box of keepsakes.

Keziah was pensive as she swept through the hall into the shop — only to be confronted by a tall, lithely built gentleman with a shock of raven-black hair and even darker eyes that were shrewdly assessing the well-stocked shelves of the apothecary. Turning on his heel, the man's full attention locked onto Keziah the instant she appeared in the arch.

'Good evening, sir,' she began, slightly taken aback by the stranger's presence and appearance. He was dressed in a style and fashion that might well be customary in the elegant society of York and Harrogate, but were rarely observed in a small northern town like Barrowby! Keziah had never set eyes upon anyone quite like him — Not even amongst Barrowby's gentry up at Castlehill.

'How may I help you?'

'I very much hope you may be able to do so, ma'am.' The stranger removed his hat, bowing formally and bestowing a white, even smile as he spoke. 'It's rather a long story, I'm afraid.'

His voice was rich and deep, bearing a soft accent foreign to Keziah's ears. Withdrawing a card from the pocket of his waistcoat, the gentleman presented it to her.

'Benedict Clay of Charleston at your service, ma'am. Do I have the honour of addressing Miss Keziah Sephton?'

2

'I — er — yes. I am she, Mr — ' She paused, her gaze falling to the card in her hands. '*Mr Clay* . . . I regret my father, the apothecary, is presently out visiting the sick, sir.'

'I am indeed sorry to have missed Mr Sephton upon this occasion. I wished to pay my respects to your father and enquire if I might visit at some convenient time during the near future? I'm bound for Scarborough, you see, and have but a few hours in Barrowby before taking the stagecoach out to the east coast.

'However, immediately my affairs there are concluded, I intend returning and putting up at the Wild Swan here in town.'

'I don't quite understand,' began Keziah slowly, holding the card between her fingers. 'How exactly we might assist you?'

'My apologies, ma'am. I'm not making a great deal of sense!' He laughed softly, his dark eyes dancing as he gazed across the polished oak counter at her. 'I believe we might be kinfolk, Miss Sephton!'

'*Kinfolk?*' she echoed in disbelief.

'My grandfather sailed from Liverpool many years ago and settled in America. I now find myself engaged upon business here in the old country and whilst here, hope to trace my roots and locate any surviving relatives I may have.'

'You believe you're kin to my father?' she queried curiously. 'He's never mentioned any relatives who went to the Americas!'

Benedict Clay responded with his easy smile. 'Actually, I believe it to be through the distaff — your mother's line, that is — our families are connected.'

'My mother passed away some years ago, sir,' she replied simply.

'Yes, I understand so. Reverend

31

Kennard told me of your loss when I visited his church yesterday, enquiring if he knew where in Barrowby I might find your family.' Benedict Clay paused. 'I'm truly sorry, Miss Sephton. My own mother was also taken far too soon. I was scarcely more than a boy.

'More than twenty years have passed, but I still miss her sorely,' he concluded, adding gently, 'Losing somebody dear is very hard, isn't it?'

'Yes.' Keziah raised her eyes to his. 'Yes, it is. At least I knew Ma well, and my younger brother has many memories of her too. Our sister, however, was but a babe in arms . . . She never knew her mother. That's the saddest part. Edith doesn't have a picture of Ma in her mind's eye to cherish.'

Clay held her soulful gaze a long moment. 'You must have been very young when you assumed the responsibility of raising your brother and sister and caring for your father and his household?'

Keziah shook her head briskly. 'Girls

are in service or working at the mills when much younger than I was then, Mr Clay! It certainly wasn't any hardship.

'We are extremely fortunate in having each other, and Pa has always worked hard to provide a comfortable home,' she concluded. 'Since my grandmother was widowed and moved from Harrogate to live here with us, our whole family has been together under one roof.'

'Are there no other relatives? No distant cousins you may've lost touch with? In Lancashire, perhaps?'

'None, so far as I'm aware,' she answered thoughtfully. 'No, I'm sure there are not. Grandmother had only two children: my mother, and a son in the Navy who was lost at sea while still young. He was unwed.'

'It would appear the sea is in both our families' blood,' he commented with a smile. 'Your lost uncle, my grandfather — and myself, also. I'm a ship-owner, Miss Sephton.

'Until relatively recently, I knew little of my English family origins. Oh, I'd heard sketchy tales of how my grandfather had grown up on a farm in a little place called Monks Quay and — '

'Monks Quay?' cried Keziah in surprise, her eyes widening. 'It's a village on the Lancashire coast, Mr Clay! That's where Grandmother's family comes from. My mother was born there!'

Benedict Clay's handsome face creased into a broader smile. 'My word, we really are starting to get somewhere, aren't we? I would be greatly obliged for the opportunity to speak with your grandmother, Miss Sephton.

'If she will do me the honour of receiving me, I'd like to show her the old Bible my grandfather's parents passed on to him before he sailed for America,' continued Benedict Clay enthusiastically. 'I imagine they were aware they'd never see their son again, and their gift of the family Bible was for him to remember them by and also to remind Rheuben who he was and where he came from.'

'I expect you're right,' reflected Keziah. 'How hard it must have been for his parents to bid him farewell at Liverpool! And how brave he was to embark alone on such an adventure — He was only a boy, I believe you said?'

'Rheuben apparently had no desire to push a plough as his father did. He longed to put to sea and explore the world.'

'Have you brought his Bible with you to England?'

'Indeed I have, ma'am. It's safely packed amongst my luggage at the Wild Swan. It has great age and is extremely fragile, as you can guess,' he went on, his eyes never straying from Keziah's slightly flushed features. 'For generations, even before my grandfather's time, the name of each child born to the family was written inside the Bible upon his christening.

'I'd be obliged to enquire if your

grandmother recognises any of those names, and to discover if she too has a similar Bible. It is quite a tradition, I believe. This writing of names in the Holy Book.'

'There isn't anything written in Gran's Bible,' considered Keziah, warming to the amiable American. 'But her Book of Hours has lots of names written inside! At least, it has the names of the *daughters* of her family. It is very old, so may be some help to your quest.'

'Book of Hours?' he queried, with a small shake of his head. 'I'm sorry, what exactly is that, Miss Sephton? I've never heard of such a thing.'

'I think the custom for giving them died out long ago, Mr Clay,' she replied. 'They're little prayer-books that used to be hand-written by nuns or monks. According to Gran, in the olden days, Books of Hours were used mostly by ladies during their daily devotions.'

'How fascinating!' he exclaimed. 'From what you've told me, I assume this book has been passed down through the *female* line of your family?'

'Yes, it's especially precious to Grandmother because it was one of Gran's own fore-mothers who actually wrote out the prayers. She was prioress of a nunnery in Lancashire. By coincidence, Gran and I were looking at the Book of Hours just before you arrived,' went on Keziah, thoughtfully considering the gentleman standing before her. Meggan Worsley would be delighted to receive him. Gran enjoyed nothing better than recollecting past times and people, and reliving her many memories . . . If Benedict Clay really was kin, well Keziah knew her grandmother would be overjoyed to discover a blood relative she hadn't even known existed!

'I'll tell my grandmother you've called, Mr Clay,' said Keziah with a polite smile. 'I'm sure she'll be delighted to meet you and hear everything you have to say about your family.'

'I sincerely hope it proves to be a family we share, Miss Sephton,' he responded graciously. 'Meanwhile, might I have the pleasure of your company . . .'

He broke off as the brass bell above the door jangled and George Cunliffe and Edith burst into the shop, laughing and breathless and bringing streams of cold damp air with them.

'I helped George feed Tinker and Beauty and put the waggon away, Kezzie!' cried Edith, her bonnet and braids flying as she raced across to her elder sister. 'Then we ran all the way from the stables!'

'I can see that!' laughed Keziah, straightening Edith's askew bonnet. 'Hurry and take off your wet coat and boots — Granny's made parkin!' she added, returning her attention to the American waiting patiently before her. 'Sorry about that, Mr Clay!'

'Not at all, Miss Sephton. If you would be so kind as to present my compliments to your grandmother and your father? I shall call again with the anticipation of becoming acquainted with them both.' He smiled, bowing slightly before replacing the fine, wide-brimmed hat. 'It's been the greatest pleasure talking to you, ma'am.

'Good evening to you!'

With a polite nod in George Cunliffe's direction and a smile for Edith, who was hovering wide-eyed in the arch, Benedict Clay quit the apothecary and disappeared into the night.

'Fhee, I've not seen his like around here before!' exhaled George, casting a suspicious glance after the American before fixing his gaze upon Keziah. 'Who the devil is he, Kez? What does he want with you?'

'Didn't he smell nice!' cried Edith, darting curious eyes from George to her sister and back again. 'Why does he talk so queer?'

'He's *foreign*, lass! Foreigners never talk like us,' replied George, his attention never straying from Keziah's becomingly flushed cheeks. 'Reeking to high heaven of bay-rum and roses

— Flashing his brass about too, I don't doubt!

'What *did* he want with you, Kez?' persisted George curtly. 'You have to watch his kind, y'know. His manner was nowt short of improper!'

'It wasn't anything of the sort!' returned Keziah crisply, bundling Edith through the arch into the hallway. 'Mr Clay has extremely refined manners. He could not have been more of a gentleman!'

'He were hard taken wi' you,' grunted George, following her. '*That* much was plain for a blind man's dog to see!'

'Oh, for goodness sake, don't be so silly!' she retorted, kneeling to unbutton Edith's boots. 'Mr Clay and I were having a very intriguing conversation, if you must know.'

'Who is he, then? More to the point, who is he to *you*?' retorted George, his square jaw set. 'What's the likes of him doing in Barrowby? What's his business here?'

'In answer to your first question, the gentleman's name is Benedict Clay. He's from Charleston, in South Carolina, so he is indeed a *foreigner*, to borrow your description,' responded Keziah tartly. 'As to the nature of his business, I believe Mr Clay owns ships.'

'He's a mighty long way from the sea!' snorted George. 'You mark my words, he'll be up to some sort of mischief. Ship-owner, indeed! He's too smarmy by half, and I can see he's turned your head right enough. You'll send him packing if you know what's best for you, Kez!'

'That's as may be, however it's hardly for me to decide,' she replied airily, hanging Edith's coat and bonnet at the foot of the stairs to dry. 'Because it's *Granny* he wishes to speak to!'

' — who wants to talk to me?' Meggan enquired, leaning heavily on her stick and peering out from around the kitchen door. 'Tea's brewed if you've time to stay for a dish, George!'

'I'll not say no, Mrs Worsley!' He

strode into the kitchen, moving across the stone flags to warm himself at the fire. 'It's more than a bit parky out there tonight!'

Keziah gave Benedict Clay's card to her grandmother and explained all about him as she poured the tea. 'He's going to come back when Pa's here to find out if he can call on you, Gran.'

'I don't recall the name *Clay*, but of course that name might've come into his family through marriage,' considered Meggan, studying the card as she sat straight-backed at the kitchen table. 'When I was a bairn, I do remember there being mention of kin who'd travelled down to Liverpool. Times were hard then, and a fair few folk did it. Some were looking for jobs in the town, but others hoped to find a ship and start a new life in the New World.'

'Like Mr Clay's grandfather! He smelled ever so nice, Granny!' chipped in Edith, biting into the sticky treacle parkin Meggan had set before her. 'He had a grey coat with fancy buttons and a red and gold scarf with a sparkly pin in it!'

'A fop is what he is!' sneered George. 'Probably never got his hands mucky in his whole life!'

'That's the way of gentlemen,' remarked Meggan sagely, sipping her tea. 'Aye, I'll see Mr Clay and gladly. I'd like to hear what happened to them folk as sailed away! He'll be interested to look at the Book of Hours, I'm sure.'

At mention of the Book of Hours, Edith's head shot up from her plate of parkin. 'Tell us the story about the lost silver, Granny!'

'Why, don't you ever get tired of hearing that old nonsense, lass?' exclaimed Meggan with a laugh, for she enjoyed relating the tale every bit as much as Edith liked hearing it. 'I've told it so often, it's threadbare! Besides, George doesn't want to hear it again.'

'Yes, he does!' insisted Edith, aiming the toe of her shoe at George's shin under the kitchen table. 'You want to, *don't you, George?*'

43

''Course I do!' he muttered, making great show of wincing. 'Always glad to hear about hidden treasure and riches beyond my wildest dreams.'

'You daft ha'porth! You're worse than the lass!' Meggan shook her head, settling comfortably into her fireside chair before commencing the old family tale. 'Many, many years ago, a kins-woman of ours — a gentlewoman of means and learning called Agatha — lost her husband to the wars. In them days, it was the way for well-off widow-women to go into a nunnery, so that's what Agatha did.

'She left her big house and went into a little priory near the sea in Lancash-ire. The sisters there worked hard, tending the sick, caring for the poor, growing their own food and baking their own bread. They were also very clever, because they could read and write and it was part of the Lord's work for them to copy sacred books — '

'Hurry up and get to the part about the lost silver, Gran!' begged Edith.

'Who's telling this story — thee or me?' admonished Meggan, pausing to sip her tea. 'Agatha had to leave her little daughter behind when she left the big house, so she began writing a Book of Hours to be given to the lass when she grew up. And that same little book has been passed down from mother to eldest daughter in our family ever since.'

'Yes, but what about the thrilling bit?' urged Edith, unable to contain her impatience. 'Tell us about the *huge* chest full of silver and jewels!'

'Well, the sisters chose Agatha to be their prioress. It was a very responsible position because as well as running the priory, she was in charge of the land, mills and farms that belonged to it,' Meggan continued, taking her time as she poured a second cup of tea. 'The priory had to give lodgings to important guests — even *royal* guests sometimes — when they were travelling through Lancashire, so Agatha had to manage that too. She was a remarkable woman!'

'We know that, Gran, but what about the squire who asked her to hide his fortune?' demanded Edith, casting an exasperated glance at George. 'That's what we want to hear about!'

'You mind your granny and let her tell the tale,' chastised George mildly, helping himself to another thick wedge of parkin. 'Remember, if Agatha hadn't been as remarkable as your gran says, the squire wouldn't have trusted her to keep his silver safe from his enemies, would he?'

Edith heaved a resigned sigh. 'Sorry, Granny.'

'Eee, don't fret o'er it, lass!' beamed Meggan. 'Anyhow, this squire was a great benefactor of the priory — that means he'd given lots of land and money to the holy sisters — and when the troubles came to Lancashire, the squire knew he'd be arrested and his property seized so him and his kin had to flee the county fast. He brought the hoard of silver and jewels in an iron-bound chest to the priory and left it in Agatha's care until his family was able to return. And if worse came to worst . . . ' She paused ruefully. 'Well, it was the squire's will his whole fortune be endowed to the priory and to the glory of God.'

'His family were caught by their enemies, weren't they, Gran?'

'Every last one of them perished,' said Meggan sorrowfully. 'Not even the bairns and womenfolk were spared. Those were terrible times in Lancashire, terrible times indeed . . . '

'The sisters kept the silver safe in the sacristy for a long time,' prompted Edith, who knew the tale by heart. 'But then something else happened!'

'King Henry VIII turned against the Church. He sent his men out destroying monasteries and nunneries, plundering their treasures and valuables.' Meggan nodded, a catch in her voice. She'd related this story scores of times, yet never failed to see in her mind's eye the horror and the bloodshed when the king's men breached the priory's doors, and violated the house of holy women . . .

'Agatha and her sisters knew fine well what the king's commissioners had done at other priories — '

'So Agatha took the iron-bound chest from the sacristy and *hid* it somewhere in the priory,' chipped in Edith eagerly, her small hands clasped together with her chin resting on her knuckles. 'The king's men didn't find it!'

Meggan looked across the table to her wide-eyed little granddaughter. One day, Edie would understand the bravery of those lone women . . . but for now, all this was still a thrilling tale of hidden treasure.

'When Agatha saw the king's men riding towards the priory,' went on Meggan with a small smile, 'the old tale goes that she quickly wrote a secret message into the Book of Hours before smuggling the book out to her daughter, who was soon to come of age.

'And we womenfolk have had that

little Book of Hours in our safekeeping ever since!'

'If *I'd* been Agatha's daughter,' cried Edith, homing in on the most exciting part, her plump face pink and shining, 'I would've searched and searched till I found the treasure!'

'It wasn't hers to seek, Edith!' reprimanded Meggan severely. 'It belonged to the priory, and the priory had been torn down by the king's men! Anyway, the daughter wouldn't have known about the fortune or the secret message, would she? Only *Agatha* knew, and she was killed . . . '

'Yes, but the treasure still hasn't been found, has it, Granny?' persisted Edith, her blue eyes sparkling. 'It's still wherever Agatha hid it — All we need do is find the secret clue in your little book!'

'It's a mysterious old family tale,' commented Keziah, bustling about the kitchen and all the while listening for the ringing of the shop's brass bell. 'That's *all* it is, pet! A fairytale! There

49

aren't really any secret messages in Gran's Book of Hours — Only prayers and psalms, written by a mother for her daughter!'

'Kezzie's right,' agreed Meggan, raising her chin and smiling at Edith. 'Nowt's left of Agatha's priory except ruins and tall tales of hidden treasure! So finish up your parkin, little lass, and away to your chores!'

'Well, *I* think that chest full of silver and jewels is *still* hidden there somewhere.' Edith's jaw jutted stubbornly as she broke her last piece of parkin into bits. 'When Kezzie has her next birthday and Gran gives her the book and I'm grown up, *I* want to go and find it!'

'Tell you what, Edie,' put in George, winking broadly to Meggan. 'For the time being, how about finding some chores to do? It's high time I wasn't here an' all — Erskine'll have my hide for bootlaces!'

'How is business at the yard, George?' queried Meggan, starting to clear the dishes. 'Reverend Kennard was telling me Stanley Erskine's not in the best of health. Do you reckon he'll sell up?'

'I do. To my way of thinking, it's only a matter of time, Mrs Worsley,' George responded grimly, rising from the table and reaching for his hat. 'Erskine's made his brass. He has no kin to pass the business on to and he's getting along in years. I reckon he's had enough of living on his own in that ramshackle old place next to the yard.

'His widowed sister has a nice house in Harrogate with all the comforts, and she's keen for him to go and keep her company there — She'll likely be only too pleased to wait on him hand and foot, too,' he finished wryly. 'If I was Stanley Erskine, I'd have already upped sticks and gone!'

'Aye, but where'll that leave you?' queried Meggan bluntly. 'You know that business backwards; could you not take over the yard?'

'I'd like nowt better — If I had

t'brass!' George snorted humorlessly. 'As is, I'll have to hope the new owner dun't bring his own man with him! Anyhow, I'd best get going while I've still a job to go to. Thanks for the tea.' He turned to the door, glancing across to Keziah at the sink. 'I'll look in tomorrow — You'll think on what I said about the church social?'

' . . . What was all that about a social at St Harmon's?' enquired Meggan, when George Cunliffe had gone on his way. 'You *must* go Kezzie! You hardly ever step out from behind that shop counter. Edith and me can look after each other for once, can't we, lass?'

Edith nodded, fetching in kindling from the yard. 'You should go, Keziah. George'd like that. He's real sweet on you!'

'That's enough of that, miss!' said Keziah, checking the pots bubbling on the range before turning toward the shop. 'After you've finished your chores, help Granny lay the table for supper.

You'd best set places for Pa and Sammy as usual —

'Although,' she murmured under her breath, disappearing once more into the apothecary, 'I doubt we'll see either of them home this night!'

3

The remainder of the week passed in like fashion. Elijah Sephton's duties at Quarry End kept him from home, while Samuel continued — in Keziah's opinion — to shirk his responsibilities to the family business and left her tending the apothecary on her own.

When the shop door finally closed behind the last customer on that bitterly cold, wet Thursday evening, Keziah sighed with relief and thankfully turned the key before snuffing all but one of the lamps.

The apothecary was always especially busy towards the end of a long winter, when the weather persisted severely cold and damp and folk required remedies for prolonged seasonal ills as well as making their regular purchases of soaps, tonics, ointments, salves, rubs and the like.

This year, however, fear of fever reaching up from the lowly dwellings amongst the derelict quarry pits and spreading into the prosperous homes of the thriving market town was bringing many more customers into Sephton's Apothecary, desperately seeking any preparations which might protect them.

In the quietude of the darkened shop, Keziah fretted about her father as she methodically tidied the counters and placed clean dust sheets across the displays of pomades and perfumes, hand lotions and facial creams. Elijah Sephton was no longer a young man, and every hour he spent amongst the sick and the dying at the almshouse and Quarry End was placing his own life at great risk. Keziah sighed heavily, probing her temples with her fingertips.

She'd been working alone in the apothecary since before first light and was so tired she could barely stand straight, yet the gnawing anxiety grew more tenacious. It was not only for her father Keziah was afraid, but for Sammy also. He'd gone out directly after breakfast and despite solemn promises to return promptly and take over in the shop, had not been seen since.

Collecting the day's takings from the drawer under the counter, Keziah moved beyond the glass-paned partition into the dispensary and perched on the high stool, emptying the cloth bag onto the desk to count up. While she *was* deeply concerned about Samuel's lack of interest in the apothecary, something far more serious had been troubling her of late. Much as it galled Keziah to admit it, Freda Sharples had been absolutely correct. Since returning from York, Samuel *had* fallen into the habit of keeping company with his old school friends from Castlehill — and a reckless, roistering bunch they were too!

Miles and Percy Baldwin and Reggie Crane belonged to Barrowby's wealthiest, most influential and respected families, but over the shop counter, Keziah heard a fair measure of tittle-tattle and was keenly aware of the notorious reputation the trio's wild ways were fast attracting. The Baldwin brothers and Crane would not be hurt by it, though. They were sons of gentlemen. Their debts and damages would quietly be paid and their transgressions forgiven and forgotten.

If Samuel were to get into trouble alongside them, however, there wouldn't be money and weight of powerful, old family influence to brush *his* misdemeanors under the carpet and extricate the boy from scandal! Samuel's reputation would be ruined. His future and prospects irreparably damaged. The shame and disappointment would wound Pa terribly . . .

Despite her troubled thoughts, Keziah continued carefully totting up the day's takings. She had a good head for figuring and Elijah had entrusted the responsibility of the apothecary's book-keeping and banking to her when she was just fifteen years of age. The ledgers were meticulously kept and accurate to the last farthing. As was her custom, Keziah double-checked the amounts before dipping her pen into the ink-well and neatly entering the day's total into the ledger. That done, she unlocked the desk drawer, took out the weekly cash-box for banking and opened it up.

There was less in the box than there should have been.

Realising she was weary and her mind might be playing tricks, Keziah slowly and carefully counted the cash-box's contents, comparing the total to the previous night's entry in the ledger. She counted it again. Then counted it thrice more. It was definitely short. Perhaps Keziah had made a mistake the night before . . . But no. *No!* Money that had been in the cash-box the previous evening was now missing. Pa never touched money from the cash-box.

That left only Samuel.

Soberly, Keziah closed up the cash-box and put it into the desk drawer, locking it securely and taking one last look around the dispensary before blowing out the lamp and going from the shop into the hallway.

Pausing at the long case clock in the corner, she opened the carved door and hung the desk key upon a little hook tucked away into the side of the walnut trunk, clicked closed the ornate little door once more, and made for the kitchen, looking in at the parlour as she passed by.

Edith was curled up at Gran's side before the fire, the keepsake box open at their feet as the pair were poring over Agatha's old book of prayers.

' . . . I wish the book was written in *English*,' Edith was saying, her head resting against the rough stuff of her grandmother's thick wool skirt. 'I'd be able to read it now, because Mrs Kennard says I'm the best reader in the whole class!'

'Samuel is the only one who can

actually read the words in the book,' Meggan replied. 'But the rest of us understand what the prayers *mean*, don't we? That's what really matters, isn't it?'

'It's not the same, though,' reasoned Edith, sitting up and helping Meggan replace the contents of the keepsake box, the tattered Book of Hours fitting neatly down to one side. 'I want to read it *properly!*'

'Now Samuel's home for good,' began Meggan, closing the lid and affectionately patting her hands across it, 'mayhap he'll teach you to read the Latin! He used to help you learn lots of things.'

'That was when I was *little*, Gran,' remarked Edith doubtfully, standing on tiptoe to slide the keepsake box up onto the shelf in the chimney corner. 'Besides, Samuel's not like he used to be. He's different now.'

From the kitchen where she was putting the finishing touches to supper, Keziah had been half-listening to the conversation drifting through from her grandmother's parlour and now drew breath to comment — then thought better of it.

Edith had hit the nail on the head, though. Samuel was different now. He never used to be so inconsiderate and selfish; so utterly careless for the feelings of others and his responsibilities to his family . . . And now there was the missing money!

A knot tightened within Keziah's stomach. She'd have to speak to Samuel immediately he returned home, at whatever the hour that might be.

' . . . Happen Sammy'll be only too pleased to teach you the Latin,' Meggan was saying to Edith. 'If you don't ask him, you'll not find out!'

The girl shrugged, twisting her braid around her forefinger. 'Suppose I could try.'

' — Supper's nearly ready, Edith!' called Keziah, not turning around from draining vegetables into the low brown sink. 'Go and get your hands washed and your hair brushed!'

'It'll be nice if Samuel helps the little lass with her reading,' remarked Meggan, coming through to the kitchen as Edith clattered away up the turned stairs. 'She's one as soaks up learning. You were like that, Kezzie. Full of questions!'

'I still am, Granny!' she responded wryly. 'It's answers I'm short on.'

'Aye, you and me both!' chuckled Meggan, carefully carrying the heavy bread board from the dresser and placing it into the middle of the table, then smoothing a crease from the cloth before disappearing into the pantry to fetch the butter-dish from the cold marble shelf.

'You're right about Edith, though,' went on Keziah thoughtfully. 'She's *very* bright for her age, and it would be wonderful if Samuel could spare some time to help her with her music and reading. She looks up to him so.'

'Always has. It was nowt short of a joy to see the pair of them singing and playing together on your ma's old piano!' recalled Meggan fondly. 'And the little lass was never happier than when Samuel'd take her for a walk along the river to show her the ducks and then carry her home high on his shoulders.'

'I'd forgotten about that!' reflected Keziah wistfully. 'Sammy's been the apple of Edith's eye since she was a baby. Always the one who could dry her tears and make her laugh.

'I *wish* he was more like he used to be, Gran,' she murmured, her head lowered to setting tureens onto the table. 'I wish Sammy wasn't always off gallivanting and would stay at home more. Be part of the family again.'

'Give him *time*, lass!' urged Meggan softly, her hand upon her granddaughter's arm in reassurance. 'He's not a boy any longer, he's a man grown and — '

'My point exactly, Gran!' cut in Keziah fervently. 'Samuel has a duty to Pa and to this family. The apothecary is his inheritance and his responsibility. He should be *here* — not racketing around town with the likes of the Baldwin brothers and Reggie Crane!'

'It can't be easy for Sammy — No, Kezzie! Let me finish,' insisted Meggan when Keziah made to interrupt. 'Your brother has had a taste of a world beyond Barrowby. Seen how some other folk live. It's mayhap turned his head a tad, but try to bear with him a while.'

'Sammy must put the shop first, Gran, that's only fair!' argued Keziah in frustration. 'He's had the luxury of studying in York for years, now it's time he buckled down to the hard work of running the apothecary!'

'Your brother's no stranger to hard work, Kezzie,' returned Meggan sternly. 'Samuel never had his nose out of his books for almost two years to get that scholarship at York.'

'York was what he wanted,' retorted Keziah, knowing she sounded petulant but somehow unable to bide her tongue. 'Samuel always ends up getting what he wants!'

'Does he?' queried Meggan mildly. 'Have a care, Kezzie! Samuel's turned his back on the future he *could* have and come back to Barrowby. Aye, the apothecary's his birthright and his duty, but try to understand it's not easy for him!'

'It's not easy for any of us, Gran,' snapped Keziah more sharply than she intended. Her grandmother never saw any wrong where Samuel was concerned! And Pa was just the same. 'I've no objections to Samuel's swanning up to Castlehill for musical evenings with his fine friends — providing he puts this family and the shop first!

'As it is, he scarcely sets foot in the apothecary,' she concluded, standing back from the heat of the oven as she took out the roast. 'He comes and goes like a guest at an inn, expecting to be waited on hand and foot and *then* helps himself to — '

Keziah clamped her lips together, not

about to mention the missing money to anyone until she'd spoken to Samuel himself. Even as she set the joint to rest, the back door opened and she heard her brother's quick step along the hallway. A moment later, Samuel's animated face appeared around the kitchen door.

'My, something smells good!' he grinned, winking across at his grandmother. 'I'm just in time, aren't I?'

'Samuel, I need a word!' Keziah called after him as he charged along the hallway to the stairs. Casting an eye over the pots on the range, she glanced back to Meggan and made to follow Samuel. 'Nothing will spoil. I'll not be a moment.'

'Kezzie, don't be too hard on him,' muttered Meggan as the door swung closed behind her granddaughter. 'Sammy'll settle — You'll see.'

Sweeping along to the end of the landing, Keziah rapped upon Samuel's door before striding into the large square room. Her brother was sprawled in the chair alongside the washstand, massaging his temples with his fingertips and looked up at her quizzically as she stood framed by the open doorway. The only illumination came from the candle Keziah was holding. She couldn't see Samuel's face clearly but had immediately noticed his overly bright eyes and flushed countenance when he'd looked in at the kitchen.

'What particular bee is buzzing around your bonnet now, Kez?' he enquired lazily, stretching his long legs out before him. 'To what do I owe this spontaneous visit to my humble apartments?'

'Don't try to be clever, Samuel. Your behaviour is neither clever nor amusing,' Keziah said sharply, closing the door behind her so their words might not be overheard. 'Where have you been?'

'I told you this morning,' he replied smoothly. 'I had an arrangement to meet friends at Castlehill.'

'You also told me you'd return to look after the shop!'

'Oh really, Kez! I've already explained — '

'You knew fine well Pa would be needed at Quarry End again today,' she cut in crossly. 'And you promised faithfully you'd be back before noon — It's now past suppertime!'

'Yes, and I do humbly apologise,' he replied contritely. 'It was most remiss of me.'

'The apothecary is *your* concern now, Samuel. Yours and Pa's equally since he signed the half-share over to you!' persisted Keziah. 'You should be here, instead of disappearing goodness knows where with the Baldwin brothers and Reggie Crane! They don't need to earn a living, but you do!

'Apart from everything else, I've been on my own all day — again! But for George collecting Edith from her lessons and fetching her safely home from the rectory this past week, I would've had to close the apothecary every afternoon because you aren't here to tend the shop!'

'George is glad to be helpful,' remarked Samuel, easing off his highly polished boots. 'Any excuse for currying favour with you.

'I am sorry, though, Keziah. Truly I am,' he went on forlornly. 'I genuinely intended returning to the shop as arranged, however when I got up to Castlehill, the Baldwins introduced me to their cousin who's presently visiting. He's apparently the youngest son and wasn't going to inherit a bean, so what does the blighter do but sail off to Africa and make his own fortune!

'Came back rich as Croesus — lucky devil! He's not much older than I, but the adventures he's had, Kez, and the incredible stories he was relating . . . I simply *had* to stay for a spot of luncheon and conversation,' finished Samuel with a sheepish grin. 'I'm afraid the entire day slipped by without my noticing.'

'From your florid appearance and the liquor on your breath,' she returned tartly, 'you've done rather more than *talk*!'

'One can't refuse such generous hospitality,' he said mildly. 'It'd be churlish and frightfully bad manners. Besides, I've never met anybody quite like this man Harris before, not even in York. He's not yet six-and-twenty, but he's travelled the world, conquered all manner of challenges and amassed a fortune!' concluded Samuel admiringly, adding quietly, 'He's done so much with his life already, Kez. It made me think about things . . . but I really *am* sorry I was so long at Castlehill!'

Keziah sighed. Hearing the boyish enthusiasm in Samuel's voice, glimpsing that unmistakable excitement in his clear eyes, she could feel her antagonism calming and the resentful anger beginning to fade. 'Sammy, providing you behave sensibly when you're with the Baldwin brothers, I don't object to your visiting Castlehill, but the apothecary *must* come first! The wellbeing of our family depends upon it.'

'You're absolutely right.' He got to his feet, pushing a hand through his mop of dark hair as he paced the high-ceilinged room overlooking the town square. 'I will attend to my duties here, Kez. I swear I will. Today was thoughtless and unforgivable.

'Where is Pa, anyway? Surely he hasn't spent the whole day at Quarry End again! I don't see why he has to shoulder the burden of helping Barrowby's sick and destitute,' concluded Samuel with an impatient shake of his head. 'He isn't the only apothecary — or physician — in the town!'

'No, but Pa is one of the few willing to help those in need without thought to his own comforts and pocket!' she replied, hesitating a moment before continuing. 'Samuel, there's something else I need to speak to you about.'

'Oh, Keziah,' he sighed wearily, not turning from looking through the window down into the busy square. 'Not more sermons! I'm exhausted *and* famished. Can't whatever it is wait until after supper?'

'No. No, I'm afraid it can't,' she said, standing stiffly with her back to the door. 'It's . . . serious.'

The hesitancy in his sister's usually forthright voice surprised Samuel rather, and he turned from the window into the room, taking off his coat and laying it across the chair-back. 'You'd best get it said and done, then.'

'Last evening after closing the shop, I counted the day's takings as usual, put the money into the cash-box ready to go to the bank at the week's end, and locked the cash-box into the desk drawer in the dispensary,' she explained awkwardly, trying to frame her words so they might not sound an outright accusation. 'However, this evening when I opened the cash-box to put in today's takings, there was less inside the cash-box than there had been last night.

'Samuel — ' her eyes sought and held his steadily across the flickering candle in the dimly lit room. ' — have you — borrowed — anything from the bank money?'

'Is that all?' he exclaimed with a short laugh, an expression of sheer relief crossing his smooth face as he rolled up his shirt sleeves and moved over to the wash-stand in the corner. 'My dear sister, your grave tone quite alarmed me! Yes, of course I took some money from the cash-box — Who else could possibly have done so?'

'Why did you not tell me, Samuel?' she cried, her temper fraying. 'Those takings are my responsibility! Did it not occur to you I'd be worried? No, of course it didn't! You should at least have had the courtesy to leave an IOU, so I'd know the amount taken and the reason it was missing!'

'I was in a hurry this morning and found myself without funds,' he explained amiably, splashing water from the pitcher into the basin. 'I simply borrowed a small sum and never thought to mention it. It was only a trifling amount after all, but I'll repay it later. My apologies if you were concerned.'

'*Concerned?*' she echoed incredulously. 'Of course I was concerned — and I cannot agree the amount missing is a trifle! Pa trusts me to take care of our family's finances, Samuel! Have you no sense of responsibility? Pa *relies* on me to balance the books, manage the household expenses and keep the banking in order. How can I do that accurately if — '

'Don't mither so, Keziah!' remarked Samuel, rubbing his face and hands dry. 'I am a partner in the apothecary now — as you're never done reminding me — It's actually my *own* money I've borrowed.'

'It's this *family's* money, Samuel!' she returned curtly, her eyes flashing in the candlelight. 'We depend upon the income from the apothecary to keep the roof over our heads and food on the table. You'd do well to remember that next time you're about to help yourself to the takings!'

'You're right, as always,' he sighed, moving from the washstand to the looking-glass and soberly meeting her reflection as she stood stiff-backed behind him. 'It was thoughtless, but I have promised to pay it back, haven't I?'

'Be sure you do.' She made to leave then paused, her hand upon the door, and glanced back. 'Before banking day please. I have to keep the accounts straight.'

'Kez,' he murmured as she made to quit the room. 'Kez — There's no cause for you to mention anything about the money to Pa . . . Is there?'

She sought his gaze but briefly before taking up the candle from the dresser and turning out onto the landing.

'Supper will be on the table directly.'

Keziah closed the door quietly, plunging Samuel's room into near blackness. He flung himself back into the chair beside the cold grey fire and expelled a heavy breath, listening to his

sister's soft footfalls along the landing
fade to silence in the tall old house.

★ ★ ★

The family was abed, and Keziah stood
alone in the back kitchen washing the
supper plates.

Pa had come home as she was
dishing up, so the whole family had
been able to sit down and eat the
evening meal together for the first time
since fever had broken out at Quarry
End. Her father had spoken little,
content merely to be in company with
his family; to watch and listen to his
children and their lively conversation.
There was no mistaking the greyness of
Elijah's countenance however, nor the
hollowness encircling his weary eyes.

After they'd finished eating, Keziah
lost no time placing a pan of hot coals
into her father's bed and heating
sufficient water so he might bathe
before retiring and soothe the aches
from his bones. When she came back

76

downstairs from putting Edith to bed, Keziah found Elijah seated in the rocking chair next to the kitchen fire, hunched forward with his elbows propped on his knees and his head bowed.

'Pa?' she breathed quickly. 'Are you unwell?'

'Hmm? Oh, no. Nay, lass! Just thinking . . . ' He smiled sadly, looking up at her. 'Counting my blessings, more like! I've such a lot to be thankful for, Kezzie.'

'We all have, Pa. 'specially at times like this.' She swallowed the lump in her throat, stirring the fire into a brighter blaze. 'Are things so terribly bad at the quarry pits?'

'Worst I've seen in a lifetime trying to doctor folks' ills, and that's saying summat!' He shook his head grimly. 'The almshouse is overcrowded like always, and fever's rife amongst the old workings. Whole families dwelling in the caves and shanties down there are falling sick . . . We're doing what we can, but it's not nearly enough.'

'You couldn't do more, Pa,' she murmured, heartsick to see the anguish etched into his haggard face. 'Nobody could.'

'This *town* could! To have folk living in the hunger and cold and filth of a place like Quarry End is an abomination, Kezzie!' declared Elijah vehemently. 'Every man in Barrowby should be hanging his head for shame at allowing such poverty on their doorsteps! We need *change* — and just one good, strong, educated man to stand up and start bringing it about!'

'Meanwhile, you and the others at the almshouse are helping in every way possible,' she whispered, seating herself upon the footstool beside his hearthside chair.

'You're a good lass, Kezzie, and you always work so very hard,' he sighed, resting a hand upon her hair and patting her head as he'd done when she was a small child. 'At least now Samuel's back, he's able to share the load. Is everything all right with the shop? You must tell me straight out if it's not, for lately we haven't had the chance to talk things over like we usually do.'

'We miss you, Pa, but everything is well,' she answered simply, smiling up at him. 'Gran is getting stronger each day and Mrs Kennard is very pleased with Edith's progress. She got the best marks in the spelling test!'

'Aye, Edith rattled off all the words when I went in to say goodnight!' Elijah's face creased into a broad beam. 'She says she's going to ask Samuel to teach her the Latin — That lass has more curiosity than a dozen cats!'

'I'll not argue with that,' chuckled Keziah. 'There never was such a child for questions! I do hope Samuel can spare some time for her, now he's home for good.'

'My, but it's grand the whole family all being together again!' exclaimed Elijah warmly. 'Your ma'd be right pleased to have Samuel back where he belongs. She worried something fierce when he won that scholarship and went to York! We both did. He was only a little lad, and for the first couple of years, he was awful miserable at that school. Your ma and me wanted to fetch him home, but Sammy was determined to stick it out.'

'I didn't know about that,' she murmured.

'Well, you were nowt more'n a bairn yourself then,' Elijah said, tamping down his pipe and touching a lighted spill to the rough-cut tobacco. 'It was a remarkable thing for a boy from a humble family to earn the chance to be educated at such a fine school. But it meant Sammy going miles away from us — living on his own, surrounded by strangers who were not of his class and bred in a world he knew nowt about.'

'I've never considered how lonely York must've been,' mused Keziah, thinking back to that day long ago, when Ma and Pa had bundled Samuel onto the coach with his box and waved him goodbye. 'To leave his family and home, and know he wouldn't see us again for a very long time must've been awful!'

'Unhappy as he was, Samuel studied hard and proved his worth. I only wish your ma had lived to know that from all the talented scholars at York, it was our Samuel who was given the prize in his final year!' finished Elijah, smiling ruefully. 'Reverend Kennard has asked him to play at Easter, you know — hearing her son playing in church on Easter Sunday would've filled your ma with such joy. Kezzie — *Such joy!*'

'I know, Pa,' she whispered, squeezing his hand. 'Granny was saying only today Samuel inherited his gift for music from Ma.'

Elijah laughed softly. 'The lad certainly didn't get it from an old heathen with cloth ears like me! Nor the brains for the education he's had. Mathematics, Greek, Latin, philosophy and all the rest of it — *Education* — that's the key to opening all doors in life, Kezzie! Our Samuel can hold his head high beside the finest gentleman in the whole county.

'I went as far with book-learning as I could, but Sammy . . . He'll be a man of substance in this town! A man others will respect and look up to. Someone who can help poor folk and make a real difference in Barrowby.'

Father and daughter talked a while longer, until Keziah gently eased the mug of tea from Elijah's clasped hands. 'You should go up and get some sleep, Pa. You can scarcely keep your eyes open — and I don't doubt it'll be another early start for you come morning.'

'Aye, true enough,' he said, rising stiffly from the rocking chair and kissing her cheek. 'Goodnight, Kezzie. Thanks for everything you do. I wouldn't like you to think I don't appreciate it, because I do.'

'I know,' she murmured, lighting and handing him his candle. 'Away upstairs now. I'll bring you some chocolate presently, and I've put out your clean shirt for tomorrow. Your coat and hat need a good brushing too; I'll see to it.'

She did so, and it was almost midnight before the day's chores were at last completed. The old house was enveloped in the quietude that settles upon a home when its occupants are slumbering, and Keziah trod softly so as not to disturb their rest. After looking in on Edith to ensure she was still warmly wrapped in her blankets, she continued along the landing and retired to her own room. Keziah had barely unpinned her thick chestnut hair and begun brushing it out when she heard a noise from downstairs.

In the shop? Or perhaps even inside the hallway —

Snuffing her candle between finger and thumb, Keziah padded across the floorboards in her stockinged feet and inched open the door. Straining her ears, she heard a muffled thud. A door swinging softly shut. There was most

certainly somebody below in the apothecary!

Mindful of not making any sound to
alert the intruder, Keziah sped along to
Samuel's room at the end of the
landing. Edging open the door, she
slipped within and closed the door
behind her, crossing the dark room
towards his bed.

'Samuel!' she hissed, reaching out a
hand to waken him. 'Samuel, wake up!
There's somebody — '

His narrow bed was empty.

Another sound came from directly
below in the shop — small, but distinct
and quite unmistakeable. It was immediately followed by the familiar dull
thump of the apothecary's heavy
glass-paned door being firmly shut.

Keziah was at the window in an
instant, flinging it open wide and
leaning out across the still.

'*Samuel!*'

His cloaked and hatted figure was
striding out across the rain-soaked
cobbled square, an arm raised in

cheerful salutation to the group of young revellers spilling from the Rose and Crown.

Either Keziah's voice was lost on the rain or her brother chose not to heed her call, for he merely continued across the square to be absorbed into the throng of merry-makers. Amid much laughter and back-slapping, the young gentlemen clambered into two waiting carriages and rattled noisily from the square, speeding away from Barrowby and up towards the Harrogate road.

Keziah could only stand watching them depart. Rainwater dripped in rivulets from her unbound hair as she drew in from the window and fastened the catch tight, but she continued staring bleakly from the rain-spattered panes into the deserted square for some considerable while longer before finally turning away. Feeling along the mantelshelf for the candle, she lit it and with heavy heart started downstairs as she knew she must.

Pausing at the foot of the stairs, she

opened the long case clock, retrieved the key from its hook within the walnut trunk and noiselessly let herself into the apothecary. Entering the dispensary, Keziah unlocked the desk drawer and hesitated, her hand trembling slightly as she reached for the cash-box. Willing herself be mistaken and her brother innocent of that which she suspected, Keziah slowly raised the lid.

The sturdy little cash-box was empty. Samuel had taken every last farthing of the week's takings.

4

' . . . I've packed the loaves for the almshouse into baskets,' Meggan said, when Keziah came through from the apothecary unfastening her apron. 'I made extra batches of oatcakes, so there's them for you to take as well.

'It's a lot for you to carry,' went on the elderly woman artfully, settling to her darning in the parlour. 'Perhaps George might give you a hand this evening, eh?'

'*Granny!*' admonished Keziah with a twinkle in her grey eyes. 'I'll manage the baskets well enough on my own, thank you!'

'I only thought . . . ' murmured Meggan innocently, leaving the sentence unfinished as she threaded a bodkin.

'I know what you thought!' returned Keziah, surveying the baskets laden with bread, oatcakes and whatever other provisions the family could spare. Meggan was correct, though. Without George's help and the use of Erskine's waggon, Keziah *would* need to make several trips down through Barrowby and out to the edge of town, where the almshouse stood amid the remnants of the old quarry workings. As well as providing for the poor living within its walls, the almshouse distributed food to infirm and needy folk dwelling in the tunnels, caves and shanties at Quarry End.

'I'll make up a basket of food and drink for Pa, too,' she decided aloud. 'Likely as not, he'll be at the almshouse all night again.'

'Is it still no better down there then?' queried Meggan in consternation.

'It's dreadful, Gran,' replied Keziah, disappearing into the cool, dark pantry. 'I don't see much whenever I deliver the food, of course, but I *hear* things! So many people have already died, and more are falling sick each day. There's little hope for any of them. All Pa can do is try to ease the suffering during their last hours.'

'Aye, fever's a bad do and no mistake,' reflected Meggan soberly. 'I've seen a fair few fevers in my time, but I reckon the worst was when I was in service at Monks Quay. I always accompanied my lady and her daughters when they went shopping to Liverpool.

'We'd set off in the carriage for one such trip and were going along the coast road when we were turned back by news that fever was raging in the port.'

'It's fortunate you heard!'

'It came aboard a tea clipper from the east. Yellow Jack, they called it,' recalled Meggan. 'The sickness spread through the grog shops and lodging houses all around the waterfront. Whole streets had to be burned to the ground to purge the town of it.'

'Thank heavens we've never had anything as bad as that here in

Barrowby!' exclaimed Keziah. 'I suppose the dangers are greater in a busy port like Liverpool — I wouldn't care to live in such a huge, crowded place.

'I wonder if Mr Clay has come from there?' she wondered as an afterthought. 'I suppose his ship must've have docked at Liverpool, mustn't it?'

'He could well be kin, you know,' mused Meggan, glancing to the mantelshelf where the American's card was propped against the jar of spills. 'In those bygone days he spoke about, life on the land was changing fast. In Monks Quay, men were losing their jobs and families being turned out of their cottages. Often times, them as could raise the money for passage went down to Liverpool and sailed off to the New World, hoping for a better future.'

'Was passage very expensive?'

'It certainly weren't cheap! Families scrimped and saved for years to get the fare. A man alone might be able to work his ticket aboard ship, though,' replied Meggan, adding thoughtfully, 'I expect that's what Mr Clay's grandfather did. I'll look forward to talking to this Benedict Clay — if he calls back, that is!'

'I'm sure he will, Granny, just as soon as he returns from Scarborough. Mr Clay struck me as utterly determined to trace his family,' replied Keziah, stoking the fire with coals and kindling so it would remain warm throughout the evening. 'He seems a thoroughly decent gentleman. Very gracious and quite elegant, too!'

'Edith was *very* impressed — The lass didn't stop talking about him for hours,' chuckled Meggan, her blue eyes twinkling. 'Although somehow, I don't think your George cottoned to our visitor!'

Keziah chuckled too. 'He's not *my* George, Granny — But you're right about one thing — George certainly *didn't* take to Benedict Clay. Thought him too fancy and flowery by far!

'Would you like a cup of chocolate

before I go to the rectory for Edith?' she added. 'Samuel's asked for a cup, so it's already heating.'

'That'd be grand — the very thing to keep the damp out of my bones!' replied Meggan cheerfully, going on quietly, 'Is everything alright between you and Samuel? These past days, you've hardly even *looked* at one another, much less spoken! What's wrong, pet?'

'It's nothing, Gran,' replied Keziah lightly, turning through into the kitchen. 'You know how it is with Samuel and me sometimes. We don't always see eye to eye.'

'Never have,' nodded Meggan sagely. 'Even as a bairn, you were the practical, reliable one while Samuel's head was stuffed full of plans and dreams!

'Sammy's a right good lad though,' she finished affectionately, fishing into the basket for more darning wool. 'Oh, I know he often tries your patience, Kezzie, but he'll settle — just give him time.'

* * *

As it turned out, Keziah was spared making several journeys back and forth to the almshouse by Alan Millet, the greengrocer whose shop was a few doors along the square from the apothecary.

She'd already fetched Edith home from the rectory, and was starting out with the first baskets when Alan's lad returned with the barrow from the last of the greengrocery's deliveries.

' . . . You're more'n welcome to borrow the barrow, Miss Sephton,' said Alan, manoeuvring the heavy vehicle alongside and holding the shafts fast while she set the baskets inside. 'I'll hang on here while you nip indoors and fetch the rest.

'Leave the barrow round back in t'yard when you're done with it — And remember me to your pa, won't you?' continued the greengrocer amiably. 'I've hardly seen him since the fever started up.'

Daylight had long since faded into bone-chilling darkness when Keziah reached the edge of town and continued along the track to cross the old stone pack bridge. It was steep and slippery and seldom used these days. Keziah needed every ounce of strength in her arms and shoulders to force the laden barrow up onto the crown, then had to grip the shafts tightly as its own weight took the barrow over and it began rolling away from her down the far side into the rutted, overgrown path out towards Quarry End.

By day, the derelict workings were a great, gaping wound gouged into the hills and valley, set about with mean dwelling places where homeless folk sought shelter. However, in the darkness of night Keziah could see none of it, and was relying upon memory and what scant moon there was to weave her way between the pits and spoil heaps towards a scarred shelf where the almshouse huddled against bare rock. As she drew nearer, Keziah was compelled to tread more carefully, pushing the heavy barrow even slower lest it overturn on the sloping, stony ground leading down to the almshouse. Fever torches were burning a short distance from the high walls of the desolate building, warning the unwary to approach no further.

Keziah proceeded between the spitting torches and tapped at a panelled door set deep within the windowless walls. A grille was duly pulled back and the almoner peered through, screwing his eyes against the torches' light to make out who stood there.

'Oh, it's you, Miss Keziah!' he greeted cheerfully. 'I'll fetch your pa.'

'Thanks, Mr Hewitt. I've brought him supper and fresh clothes, and some provisions.'

'So I see! We're much obliged,' he said, eyeing the baskets. 'These poor devils need all the charity they can get. I'll not be long bringing your pa, miss.'

Keziah nodded, propping the shafts of the barrow upon one of the old wind blocks. Flexing and stretching her aching shoulders and arms, she gazed up to the starless night sky. Smuts and sparks of cinder and fire were spitting from the torches, exploding into the air to be snuffed by a cold mist descending from the surrounding hillsides. Keziah closed her eyes tightly and willed Pa to come out soon. The acrid smell of smoke did little to mask the stench of sickness and death permeating the very timbers and stones of the almshouse —

She jumped at the rasp of bolts being drawn back. The panelled door was pulled open a little way and Elijah Sephton had no sooner stepped out than Keziah flew to him, hugging him fiercely.

'Oh, Pa!'

'Eh, what's all this about then?' he asked mildly, patting the crown of her bonnet. 'Is owt wrong at home?'

She shook her head, biting her lip and struggling to gain a grip on the overwhelming rush of emotion. Her father was a modest man of comfortable figure and kindly features, and to see him looking like this — so old and gaunt and tired — was more painful than Keziah's tender heart could bear.

'Everything's all right at home,' she gasped, anxious he shouldn't be worried. 'Samuel's looked after the shop today and we're all well. It was only . . .'

'Aye, I know, pet.' he sighed heavily. 'I know! Thanks for coming here regular like you do and bringing the provisions. It's been a hard winter and it's not over yet by a long chalk! There's folk living down here in the quarry who'd starve without the victuals they're given from the almshouse.'

Keziah nodded, gazing up into his haggard, unshaven face. The strain of past weeks appeared to have taken its toll all of a sudden, for Pa seemed years older than when she'd seen him last. There was a desperate weariness about his eyes tonight; the dear face that so readily creased into kindly smiles was now grey and drawn into deep furrows.

For the first time ever, Elijah appeared small and vulnerable to Keziah's eyes, and her heart ached with the sharp realisation of how little she could do to help him and how very, very easily her father might be taken from them by the fever that had already claimed so many lives in Barrowby.

'You — you look all in,' she mumbled thickly.

'I feel worse'n I look, and that's saying something.' He smiled over the tops of his spectacles at her, adding soberly, 'It's been a rough day. One of the worst. I can't linger, pet. I've to get back in. There's folk waiting.

'Borrowing Alan Millet's barrow for the provisions was a grand idea,' Elijah went on, moving toward the laden vehicle. 'Let it stand here though; I'll take the provisions inside. I don't want you coming any nearer than you've need to.'

Between them, they unloaded the

baskets and boxes and Elijah relayed them through the doorway into the body of the almshouse while Keziah remained a distance away with the barrow. While she waited, her ears caught snatches of muffled voices carrying clear on the cold night air from the unseen inhabitants down amongst the quarry's old huts and hollowed-out workings. And all the while, the cries and moans of a fever victim's dying delirium reached out to her from the depths of the almshouse's infirmary.

Keziah was shuddering uncontrollably, loath to leave her father in this wretched place yet at the same time desperate for the task to be completed so she might be gone and away home.

'How's Samuel getting on in the shop?' asked Elijah breathlessly, emerging from the almshouse to bid her farewell. 'He must be a big help to you.'

Keziah's lips compressed. She wouldn't hurt Pa by telling him what

Samuel had done, nor that until today he'd spent many more hours gallivanting with his Castlehill friends than he had behind the apothecary counter. She gave the only favourable remark she could truthfully make about her younger brother's conduct. 'Samuel is very conscientious with our customers. He listens to all they have to say about their ailments and pays each person great attention. Everybody seems to hold him in very high regard.'

'Aye, he's a fine lad and mark my words, our Samuel'll make summat of himself in the town!' beamed Elijah. 'I knew once — '

He broke off, turning at the rattle of waggon wheels turning past them around to the yard with its tall blind walls running along three sides of the almshouse. 'You'd best be on your way, Kezzie. We'll be bringing folk out presently.'

She nodded rapidly, understanding with a jolt the import of her father's quiet words. The almshouse was about to release its dead.

'It's not a pleasant sight and I'd rather you didn't see it.' Elijah turned to the bolted panelled door, knocking to be admitted but pausing to look back at his daughter. 'Thank you for what you do, Kezzie. It's not an easy life for a young lass — '

'It's the life I like and the life I want!' she returned earnestly, wanting to run to the comfort of his embrace again. 'I'd not choose any other!'

She stood and watched his stooping shoulders bow to enter the solid little door, and heard the bolts bang home behind him. That Pa was risking his own life tending the sick and dying was more than Keziah could face up to just then. Snatching the shafts of the barrow, she started purposefully upon the long walk home.

However, she'd barely reached the pack bridge when the waggon loaded with emaciated cadavers swathed in coarse shrouds trundled past. Dragging the barrow aside, she hurriedly covered her nose and mouth, barely able to stifle nausea as the waggon rumbled on and over the bridge, its nameless dead borne into the darkness for burial.

5

Banking day was fast approaching.

Keziah had kept her word and remained silent, but despite Samuel's solemn promise, he'd returned not a single shilling of the missing money. Indeed, her brother was behaving as though nothing untoward had occurred. She didn't know what to do. Worst of all, her covering for him was enabling Samuel to evade the consequences of stealing from his own family. He'd also succeeded in making Keziah an accomplice to his wrongdoing.

Consulting the neatly written shopping list as she hurried along Caxton Street, Keziah was still seething from an encounter with Samuel earlier that morning. Pa had been in the apothecary making up medicines and Samuel had won him over with some tale or other, the outcome being that Samuel had dressed in his best and disappeared, ignoring Keziah's protestations.

She resented being —

'Are you following me?'

The gloved hand whipped out from around the corner of the ginnel and fastening around Keziah's lower arm, dragged her away from the main street, and shoved her shoulders back against the alley's wall.

'*Spying* on me?'

'Don't be ridiculous!' snapped Keziah, her momentary shock replaced by anger and indignation. She shook free of her young brother's grip. 'What on earth do you think you're doing — ?' She broke off, her eyes narrowing suspiciously as she searched his face. 'You're up to something, Samuel! I overheard you telling Pa you were seeing Reverend Kennard this morning — so why are you skulking around Caxton Street, instead of being at St Harmon's?'

'What I do and where I go is none of your concern, Keziah!' he retorted. 'I *saw* you following me, and I refuse to be spied upon!'

'You have a guilty conscience, my lad!' She shook her head in disgust. 'Do you care nothing for the truth anymore? Heaven knows you've always had your faults, but hitherto at least you were honest! What's *happened* to you, Samuel? What sort of a person have you become to steal from your family and deceive your own father?

'Is there a single grain of truth in your promises to repay the takings? Or is that just another in your endless catalogue of falsehoods?'

'The money will be repaid,' he returned coldly. 'I've already told you that.'

'You've told me lots of things!' she countered sceptically. 'You're so often in your cups when you come creeping home from the Rose and Crown, I doubt you have any recollection of what you do tell me!'

'You've a harsh tongue, Keziah,' he commented, turning from her gaze. 'I wonder how George Cunliffe puts up with such a sour pill!'

Keziah's face flared but she did not rise to the taunt. 'You're even now deceiving Pa because *he* believes you're at church — Don't you *care* about that either?'

'Of course I care!' he blurted, his composure suddenly crumbling. 'Whether you believe it or not, I *am* sorry. Truly I am. Especially about lying to Pa.

'You haven't — *said* — anything to him, have you?'

'*I* don't break my promises!'

'Thank you for that,' murmured Samuel, suddenly looking vulnerable and afraid. 'I've put you in a wretched position, I own that. I really am grateful for your not giving me away, Kezzie.'

'I don't want your gratitude,' she retorted, forcing back the wave of sympathy she was feeling for her troubled young brother. 'I've held my tongue not for your sake, but for Pa and Gran's.

'They have faith in you, Samuel!

They'd be terribly hurt and bitterly disappointed if they knew the truth. You need to think on that and quickly mend your ways,' concluded Keziah solemnly. 'You must put back the money before banking day. If you don't, then I won't lie to save you.'

'You won't need to, Kez!' he exclaimed earnestly. 'I'll have every penny by then. I have a certain — '

'I don't want to hear about your schemes, Samuel,' she cut in crisply. 'Just make sure the takings are returned in full.'

Briskly adjusting her rain-soaked bonnet, Keziah turned on her heel and strode out from the ginnel and along Caxton Street to continue her errands.

★   ★   ★

When she emerged from the draper with a bulky parcel of flannelette for new nightgowns, the driving rain had turned to sleet, slanting across from the distant hills and crusting the jagged edges of the castle battlements with grey ice before swirling down into the town. Keziah paused upon the draper's threshold, arranging the parcel with her other purchases and tightening her bonnet strings before bowing her head and stepping out into the teeth of the bitter weather.

'Good day to you, Miss Sephton!'

Glancing up, she was startled to find Benedict Clay at her side. He raised his hat with customary politeness, smiling down at her.

'Those packages look rather unwieldy. May I help you with them?'

'Oh, good morning, Mr Clay! Really, I can manage — ' she began, but he was already relieving her of the basket and parcels. 'Well, thank you! It's very thoughtful.'

'Not at all. It's my pleasure to be of assistance, ma'am,' he replied amiably, falling into step beside her as they proceeded along Caxton Street. 'Where is your next port of call?'

'The dairy. Then the tobacconist,

iron-monger and haberdashery — I'm afraid I've only just started the day's shopping, Mr Clay,' she replied, her eyes laughing up at him. 'I truly can manage on my own, you know!'

'I don't doubt it for an instant, Miss Sephton! However, I'd deem it an honour to accompany you and actually — ' He paused, taking Keziah's arm to steady her footing over the slippery cobbles as they crossed the busy street. ' — it's fortuitous we've bumped into one another, because I'd be most grateful if you'd consider doing me a great favour?'

She turned to him enquiringly, but they had reached the dairy and Benedict Clay dutifully followed Keziah inside as she continued her round of errands. It wasn't until they were at the haberdasher's, and she was standing waiting while the assistant measured and cut ribbons, that Keziah became aware of the interest a strikingly handsome and obviously wealthy stranger like Benedict Clay was arousing amongst the matrons in the cramped haberdashery — not least because he was in the company of the apothecary's homely spinster daughter!

She glanced at him sidelong as she considered the selection of buttons arranged in the case before her. Benedict Clay was handsome, there was no doubt about that! His tanned skin and wavy hair, blue-blacker than a raven's wing and worn longer than was customary in Barrowby, together with the exquisitely tailored clothes and his rather old-fashioned, leisurely demeanour certainly set the well-mannered American apart from local folk. Then there were his eyes. Those intelligent, intuitive dark eyes . . . The darkest, warmest eyes Keziah had ever seen, with that beguiling sparkle igniting deep within them whenever he smiled —

'Five-and-twenty of the hooks, was it, miss?'

'Hmm?' The assistant's enquiry cut into Keziah's reverie. 'Oh, yes. Yes. Five-and-twenty. And buttons . . . I need buttons . . . '

When they quit the haberdashery and Keziah's errands were at last complete, Benedict Clay paused on the sidewalk, looking up and down the wide arc of shops. 'May we talk a moment, Miss Sephton? Perhaps you would join me for coffee? I believe I've seen a café around here somewhere.'

'Pearce's tea-room, yes. It's just over there.' She indicated across the bustling crescent to a double-fronted establishment with shining, brightly lit windows and snow-white lace curtains. 'On the corner, opposite the bank. Earlier, you mentioned a favour, Mr Clay. How may I help you?'

'I'll explain,' he began, taking Keziah's arm and guiding her between the throng of carriages, carts, waggons and drays weaving up and down the wide, sweeping thoroughfare. 'I returned on the stage from Scarborough late last evening. My business there is concluded. As you know, I am checked into the Wild Swan hotel, and propose staying in Barrowby while I endeavour

111

to discover more about my English family — Ah, here we are!'

Pearce's tea-room was genteel and very expensive. Although Keziah occasionally bought tea or chocolate as special treats for Pa or Granny from the adjoining well-stocked shop, she'd rarely been into the tea-room itself — and only then, upon special days. As she and Benedict Clay were shown to a secluded, prettily set little table, Keziah recalled with a pang of nostalgia how Pa had always brought the whole family here for tea on her mother's birthday. The bittersweet emotions those long-ago happy memories evoked must've shown on Keziah's expressive face, for as they settled around the circular corner table with its crisp white linen and fine eggshell porcelain, Benedict Clay leaned toward her in concern.

'Is anything wrong, Miss Sephton?' he asked quietly. 'Of a sudden, you look downcast.'

'I'm quite well, thank you.' She hesitated, searching her companion's serious eyes before going on. 'It's just, well, my father used to bring us here to celebrate Ma's birthdays. I haven't been in the tea-room since she passed away.'

'I'm so sorry to have stirred painful memories,' he responded gently, making to rise. 'You'd prefer to leave, of course — '

'Not at all!' she interrupted with a smile, arresting his arm with a light touch. 'Please, do be seated. I can't deny feeling a sadness, coming in here and thinking back, but oh, mine are very happy memories, Mr Clay! They are always welcome.'

'I'm glad,' he replied, pausing from their conversation as a waitress in a neat black dress and frilled white cap took their order for coffee and pastries. 'Miss Sephton, I've become aware your grandmother is presently not in the best of health. That being the case, I'm mindful of not tiring her during my proposed visit.'

'That's most considerate, Mr Clay, however Granny is much stronger these days and you need not worry about your visit having anything other than a beneficial effect,' replied Keziah, pouring the fragrant coffee. 'Family means everything to Gran and she gets enormous pleasure from recalling the old times in Lancashire. She's looking forward to meeting you and insists you stay for tea afterwards — So you see, you simply must come!'

'If you're certain, then I shall be delighted!' He beamed at her. 'In truth, I would have been terribly disappointed not to have had the opportunity of meeting Mrs Worsley and the rest of your family. Nonetheless, I wonder if you and I might discuss our family backgrounds a little? In this way, I can listen to whatever your grandmother has to tell me without troubling her by asking lots of unnecessary questions.'

'Yes, that makes sense,' agreed Keziah, a dainty silver fork poised above the light-as-air almond slice upon her plate. 'I'll be pleased to relate everything I know. And of course, I'm very interested to hear more about your side of the family.'

'Unfortunately, I don't have much to tell,' he answered soberly. 'My grandfather died long before I was born, however as I understand it, he came from farming stock on the coast of Lancashire. When he was little more than a boy he sailed from Liverpool aboard a barque bound for Virginia.'

'Did he ever return to England?'

'Not as I'm aware. However, he was a seaman his whole life, so it's highly probable some of the ships he served aboard docked at English ports. Grandfather made America his home, though. Took a wife and raised a family in Virginia. His daughter was my mother. She married a timber-man and moved further inland.'

'Do you have brothers and sisters?'

Benedict shook his head. 'My three sisters and only brother perished with our mother when our homestead was attacked and burned out by marauders.

'I was twelve years old,' he continued briskly when Keziah drew breath and would have spoken. 'We lived high in the hills. My father made his living cutting lumber and had built a small sawmill alongside our house.

'He'd recently secured a substantial order for timber from a construction company in Williamsburg, so he and I went away upriver on a felling trip. We returned two weeks later to find our family laid to rest in the churchyard.'

'Benedict — I'm so very sorry . . . ' was all Keziah could say, but her eyes brimmed with compassion as they met his.

He held her gaze wordlessly before continuing at length. 'My father never recovered from losing them. He'd always been a quiet man, but after that he withdrew even deeper into his own thoughts. He gave up the mill and moved to town. Shortly afterwards, I signed aboard a ship bound for Portugal and went to sea.

'Father and I didn't meet again for years. Indeed, it wasn't until I established myself in Charleston that we were finally reunited. He was very old by then. Time was short, and my father began reminiscing about his youth; how he'd met and married my mother and so forth. Soon before he died, he gave me her sewing tin. He'd salvaged it from the ashes of our old homestead. Mother had kept family papers, letters and suchlike in the tin and when I read them, I realised any family I had left would be found here in England. In the old country. I set about making extensive enquiries, and they've led me here. To Barrowby, and to you.'

'I now understand the importance of your quest, Mr Clay,' murmured Keziah sorrowfully, gazing across into the dark eyes that were studying her intently. 'You're alone in the world.'

'No place to call home, and no one to go home to!' He expelled a resigned sigh. 'Oh, I have a house and my company offices in Charleston, Miss Keziah, but I don't *really* belong anywhere. I'm hoping this trip will change that, and I'll someday find real roots.'

'I'll be very glad to help in every way I can. We all will.'

'You're exceedingly kind, ma'am. I appreciate your taking such trouble.' He reached into his pocket and withdrew a fold of thick paper, shifting his chair nearer Keziah's so he might spread the document onto the table amongst the cups and plates. 'I'd willingly give up everything I've built in Charleston to truly belong somewhere.'

The little map he unfolded was simply drafted and depicted the Lancashire coastline. The port of Liverpool, Chester and Lancaster were marked in bold script, and prominent features such as rivers, meres, manor houses, churches, mills and other significant local landmarks were roughly sketched in.

'There's Monks Quay!' exclaimed Keziah, pointing a fingertip. 'That's where Granny comes from! My mother was born and grew up there until her family moved to Harrogate.'

'I believe my grandfather came from Monks Quay. His parents were tenant farmers for the squire who lived there — ' Benedict indicated a large house surrounded by park and woodland. ' — at a manor house named Whiteladies Grange.'

'Whiteladies! Oh, I've heard of that, Mr Clay!' cried Keziah excitedly, her eyes shining. 'Granny was telling Edith about the manor house that evening you came to the shop — Gran was in service at Whiteladies Grange when she was young. The squire and his lady gave her a beautiful little burr walnut table as a wedding present. Then years later, my mother went into service at Whiteladies, too!'

'Our families are linked by this manor house then,' he mused, sipping his coffee. 'Whiteladies Grange! Such a curious name, isn't it?'

'According to Gran, the manor house was named after a nunnery whose sisters wore robes woven from undyed wool,' went on Keziah enthusiastically, bending her head to study the map better. 'I recall her mentioning a place called Nowell Abbey, too — The manor house at Nowell was also built upon monastic ruins.'

'There are — or were — quite a number of religious houses in that part of the country,' remarked Benedict Clay, indicating other markings. 'An abundance of priories, abbeys and churches concentrated in a relatively small area. Although it's true the connections we share with Whiteladies Grange and Monks Quay might be coincidence, I'm beginning to believe there's a powerful probability we're kin, Miss Keziah!'

She saw the hope burning deep within Benedict's dark eyes, and was touched by his obvious longing to be part of a loving family again.

'While Granny was in service at Whiteladies, she often had occasion to travel into Liverpool accompanying the lady and her daughters upon outings, so she knew the town around the time your grandfather must have sailed for America. By all accounts, it was an exciting, colourful place — but Granny will enjoy telling you about that herself!'

'I can't thank you — and your family — enough for being so hospitable and helpful to a stranger,' he murmured, refolding the map and offering it to her. 'I have these details fixed into my mind, so perhaps you'd like to keep this map? It's quite an old one, drawn in a quaint fashion. Your father and grandmother may be interested to see it.'

'I'm sure they will, and thank you.' She accepted the map, carefully placing it into her basket. 'I'm afraid I really must be on my way, Mr Clay. Although Pa is in the apothecary this morning, he has need to go out to Quarry End at least twice each day to do his rounds and visit the fever patients.'

Sleet had given over to stair-rods of persistent grey rain when they emerged smiling and chatting from Pearce's tea-room, starting along the busy crescent —

'*Keziah*!'

The strident shout rang out behind them and both Keziah and Benedict Clay halted in their tracks, turning around to witness George Cunliffe vaulting from Erskine's waggon and charging towards them.

'Keziah — What are you doing?'

Her jaw dropped in disbelief.

'I would have thought that obvious!' retaliated Keziah, bridling at the sheer indignity of hearing her name yelled in the street. 'I've been doing errands and now return to the apothecary!'

George's face was set, his thin mouth set into a straight line. 'I saw you coming out of Pearce's *with him!*'

Keziah flushed to the roots of her hair but before she could utter another word, Benedict Clay took control of the situation.

'Then clearly there is little amiss with your powers of observation, sir,' he remarked easily, offering Keziah his arm and leading her away from where George stood stock-still, blocking the pavement and causing the stream of passersby to detour around him, some glancing back curiously at the ill-assorted trio.

'If you'll excuse us, we'll continue on our way. Good day to you.'

'Who do you think — '

However George Cunliffe's protest trailed behind the couple as they swept along the busy street and around the corner from his sight.

'I can't apologise sufficiently for George's appalling behaviour,' murmured Keziah, shamefaced and unable to look Benedict Clay in the eye. 'I can't *believe* he made such a scene!'

'He's the young man I saw when I called at your father's apothecary, I believe?' enquired Clay amiably, escorting her along the crowded, rainswept pavement. 'Please don't give the incident another thought, Miss Keziah. I can sympathise with his discomfort. He clearly misinterpreted the situation and

I imagine in his place, I too would feel aggrieved. The gentleman is your intended, I take it?'

'He is not!' she returned sharply. 'George Cunliffe is a dear friend of my family, that is all!'

'My apologies, Miss Keziah,' the American replied genially, opening the door of the apothecary so she might enter before him. 'It appears I too misinterpreted the situation.'

Peculiarly flustered, Keziah did not reply as they went within and was somewhat taken aback to see Samuel diligently working at her father's side in the dispensary beyond the glass partition at the rear right-hand corner of the shop.

Had her brother at last come to his senses?

'Pa,' she began, 'this is Mr Benedict Clay, the American gentleman I was telling you about.'

'Oh, how do you do, sir!' exclaimed Elijah Sephton with a broad smile, coming around the partition and extending his large hand to the stranger. 'My mother-in-law's talked of little else since Kez told us you were searching for your family!'

'I'm eager to speak with Mrs Worsley, sir, and of course hoping to find evidence we are indeed kinfolk,' responded Benedict Clay, clasping the older man's hand heartily. 'It's an honour to meet you, Mr Sephton! Your daughter has suggested it might be convenient I visit on Wednesday afternoon?'

'Aye, aye. Fine if it suits you,' beamed Elijah. 'I can't promise to be here myself, as I'm a bit tied up what with one thing and t'other, but Kez'll look after you right enough. It'll be grand if you *are* related, Mr Clay, because aside from us and her widowed brother-in-law back in Lancashire, Meggan believed her family all gone and that has grieved her sorely.'

'Until recently, I was of similar mind myself,' admitted Benedict Clay sympathetically. 'Miss Keziah and I have just now been discussing the same over morning coffee. On Wednesday afternoon, I'll bring my mother's papers and what few details I've gathered about my roots in Lancashire.'

'Meggan will be right interested in whatever you have to show her,' went on Elijah. 'She's got a box full of family stuff, so I reckon the pair of you'll have plenty to talk about!'

'That'll suit me fine, sir!' Clay laughed, his tanned features animated. 'Are you from Lancashire also, Mr Sephton?'

'Me? Nay! A Yorkshireman born and bred!' grinned Elijah. 'I was working in Harrogate — an apprentice, like — when I met my late wife. Some years after we were wed, I got the chance to move over here to Barrowby and set up my own shop.' He turned, proudly beckoning Samuel from the dispensary. 'You'll not have met my son, will you?

'Samuel's not long finished his studies in York, Mr Clay. He's come home to take up his share of the family

126

business. We're partners now, my son and me!'

'You've travelled a great distance to trace your family, Mr Clay,' remarked Samuel, stepping forward and taking Benedict Clay's hand, eyeing the patent wealth and success of this worldly man. 'I hope your trip proves worthwhile.'

'I have frequent business with Liverpool and other English ports,' replied Benedict smoothly. 'When I discovered a possible connection between our two families, I promised myself upon my next voyage to this country I would stay a while and try finding — '

The brass bell jangled and a harassed-looking woman surrounded by several small children hurried inside the apothecary.

'I mustn't detain you further,' concluded Benedict politely, his gaze briefly meeting Keziah's as he turned to quit the establishment. 'Until Wednesday, then? Good day, Mr Sephton. Samuel. Please do give my compliments to Mrs Worsley. And thank you again, Miss Keziah!'

With that, Benedict Clay was gone. Pa greeted his customer and Samuel moved unobtrusively back to the dispensary. Keziah hastened through the arch into the house, setting down the packages and shedding her wet cloak and bonnet before looking in at the parlour, where Meggan was seated at the fireside, her rosewood box open on her lap.

'Hello, Granny — I'm back! My word, but it's cold — ' began Keziah, breaking off as Meggan slowly raised her face and looked around, her eyes troubled. 'Gran, whatever's wrong?'

'Have you seen my little book anywhere, Kezzie?' she murmured anxiously, her voice trembling slightly as her questing fingers yet again searched the confines of the rosewood box. 'Edith and George and me were only looking at it after church this past Sunday, but now I can't find it!'

'Isn't it in your keepsake box?' asked

Keziah gently, crossing the room to her grandmother's side and slipping her arm about the elderly woman's narrow shoulders. 'Perhaps it's slipped down amongst the other things?'

Meggan shook her head vehemently. 'I *always* put the Book of Hours down the side here — you know I do, Kezzie! — I keep it next to the music and your grandpa's watch.

'But it isn't here, so I must've put it somewhere else, mustn't I? But I don't know where! Whatever's wrong with me, lass?' she implored, her eyes suddenly filling with tears. 'Why can't I *remember* where I've put it?'

'Oh, Granny! Don't worry!' Keziah dropped to her knees before Meggan's chair, taking both her grandmother's thin hands into her own.

The small book of prayers and psalms which had been passed down from mother to eldest daughter through many, many generations of Meggan's family was the elderly woman's dearest possession, and part of a solemn promise she'd made to her own daughter shortly before her death.

'Your book's been misplaced, that's all. It'll turn up; you'll see! Meanwhile, I'll get the kettle on straight away while we have a good think about where it can be.'

'Away, lass! I can see to making the tea while you get yourself dried off and warm,' replied Meggan practically, closing the lid of the keepsake box and rising stiffly from the fireside before starting through into the kitchen. 'Who was that talking to your pa in the shop?'

'Our American cousin!' replied Keziah, removing her coat and boots and following her grandmother into the square, stone-flagged kitchen. 'We bumped into each other in Castle Crescent and Benedict treated me to coffee and a pastry at Pearce's. We had a long talk about our families.'

'He'll be interested to see our Book of Hours.' Meggan's face clouded. 'I *do* hope I can remember where I've put it, Kezzie!'

'We'll find it, Granny,' she reassured confidently, disappearing into the pantry with the basket of butter, cheese, eggs and milk. 'Mr Clay's coming to see you on Wednesday afternoon, and was very pleased to be invited to stay for tea.'

'Suppose he really is family, Kezzie,' murmured Meggan, her eyes brightening. 'Oh, wouldn't it be grand finding somebody who's our kin after so many years?'

'Mr Clay is bringing some of his mother's belongings,' explained Keziah, reaching into her bag and withdrawing the bulky fold of thick paper. 'Meanwhile, he's given us this old map of Lancashire. Look, Whiteladies Grange is drawn on it!'

As the water bubbled towards boiling, the two women pored over names and places that had once been familiar to Meggan, while Keziah related everything Benedict Clay had told her about Monks Quay, his grandfather and losing almost his entire family in the fire at their homestead.

'Poor lad!' Meggan shook her head. 'No wonder he's so keen to find kinfolk! Being alone in the world without anybody to call your own — Dun't bear thinking about.'

'No, it doesn't,' agreed Keziah, adding ruefully, 'I must admit, I hadn't thought how terribly lonely life must be for Mr Clay!'

'The sea *is* a lonely life for a man,' remarked Meggan. 'A hard one, too. My father always said as much. He came ashore for good when he married Mother, but my brother, Amos, drowned when his boat went down sailing into Liverpool harbour. It foundered on the sand bars and all hands were lost. Then my boy Jimmy — he would've been your *uncle* Jimmy, had he lived — was killed in the Navy when he was only Samuel's age. His ship was shot to pieces.'

Even after nearly forty years, the memories of receiving a letter saying her son had died bravely in some distant sea battle, and of having stood helpless on the shore at Monks Quay watching her younger brother drowning so near to safety and yet so far from reach, came rushing back to Meggan with shocking clarity — recollections still powerful enough to bring the sharp pain of sorrow and aching loss.

Keziah went to her grandmother, gently drawing her close. 'Seafaring brought much sadness to your family . . . You and Grandpa and Ma must've been glad to leave the coast and come to Yorkshire.'

Meggan roughly dried her eyes with her handkerchief. 'Aye, that job at the hotel in Harrogate came along for your grandpa at just the right time. We settled in straight away, and had many happy years there. It was in Harrogate your ma and pa met too, so all in all, it's lucky we *did* move there, eh pet?'

Keziah smiled, going on seriously, 'Isn't Fate a curious thing though, Gran? The way a simple thing like changing your place of work can spread like ripples in a pond and change so many other things!'

'A moment can change a lifetime, Keziah. That's the wonder of it.' Meggan nodded and added with a sigh, 'Or the tragedy of it, depending on how things work out.

'You said Mr Clay's calling on Wednesday afternoon? I'll have everything ready to show him. I do hope the book turns up though, Kezzie!' she fretted, taking cups and plates from the dresser. 'Your ma entrusted it to my safekeeping, and I'll never forgive myself if I let her down and can't pass it down to you on your birthday.'

'It's bound to turn up, Granny,' reassured Keziah calmly, drying her hands. 'I'm asking Pa to come through for some tea before he sets off to Quarry End.'

Meggan nodded, watching Keziah tying on her shop apron once more. 'Are you going to go to that social with George? It should be a grand night, with the music and recitals.'

'I promised Mrs Kennard I'd help set

out the tables so I must go — but I very much doubt George and I will be going together!' grimaced Keziah, quickly explaining the unfortunate scene outside Pearce's tea-room. ' . . . I can't *believe* he shouted after me in the street that way! It was nothing short of a disgrace. People were turning around and staring at us. Whatever was he thinking to behave in such coarse fashion, Gran? George is usually so placid!'

'Still waters, lass,' commented Meggan gently. 'Can you not understand he was jealous — and hurt — when he saw a gentleman walking out with you from the tea-room? George is sweet on you, Kezzie. Always has been. You've a sharp tongue, but don't be too hard on him! He's a good man, with ambition and solid plans for the future. You'll not find better in a husband.'

'You make it sound as if we're already promised!' she countered indignantly.

'Aren't you?' Meggan met her grand-daughter's eyes keenly. 'Mayhap not in so many words, but . . . If you're not fixing to marry George, you need to set the poor lad straight! It's not fair stringing him along, Keziah.'

'Stringing him along?' she echoed, aghast. 'Granny, I've never done or said — '

'It's none of my business, lass.' Meggan silenced her with a raised hand. 'It's between the pair of you, but tread careful for otherwise you'll hurt him badly!'

Her mind spinning, Keziah went through into the apothecary. 'Pa, I've made tea and there's bread and cheese and brack on the table. You need to eat something before you go out to Quarry End. It'll likely be another long night at the almshouse —

'Where do you think you're going?' she demanded of Samuel, from the corner of her eye catching sight of him putting on his great coat. 'I thought you were staying in the shop today?'

'Have to go out for a while,' he replied airily, taking a tablet of their finest lily-of-the-valley soap and slipping it into his pocket before glancing to his father, who was dispensing a sleeping draught. 'That's alright, isn't it Pa?'

'Aye, away you go, lad!' replied Elijah, without looking up from his work. 'Mind you go easy on the ale at the Rose and Crown and don't touch any of the hard stuff. And don't stay out too late. Remember, you've work in the morning!'

The brass bell above the door jangled and Samuel swaggered out into the cold evening air.

'He knows he can get away with anything he likes, Pa,' snapped Keziah, her mouth tight. 'Samuel plays on your good nature.'

'He's nobbut a lad, Kezzie!' admonished Elijah mildly, weighing out ingredients. 'After the kind of life he's caught sight of in York, it's bound to be hard for Samuel to knuckle down to running an apothecary in a small town like Barrowby.'

'Knuckle down?' she blurted incredulously, not adding that if she were a partner in the family business she'd make much of such a tremendous gift! 'Samuel ought to be thankful for this opportunity, instead of constantly shirking his responsibilities!'

'He'll settle, lass. Be patient — Give the boy time.'

The sheer injustice of the situation burned fiercely within Keziah, and she longed to speak out — tell their father exactly what his precious son and heir had been up to — but Keziah bit back the bitter words. Not to protect Samuel, oh no, but to spare Pa's feelings and preserve the immense pride he felt in his only son's accomplishments. She couldn't bear the notion of Elijah's being distressed by discovering Samuel was taking — *stealing* — the family's money and indulging in foolishness with his cronies from Castlehill.

'Samuel should be here, Pa,' was all she said.

'Be patient with him, Kezzie! He's young still — and so are you,' Elijah said gently. 'There's not so many years separates the pair of you in age, but when your ma fell sick, *you* had to grow up before your time. You took on worries and burdens a young girl shouldn't have had to bear.

'But try not to grow *old* before your time, lass,' he urged quietly. 'Don't forget what it is to be young!'

Keziah didn't trust herself to speak. Fuming, she bustled from the dispensary into the shop as the jangling bell announced another customer. Samuel was the one at fault — Samuel was the irresponsible, deceitful one — So why was Pa criticising *her?*

Presently, Elijah began preparing for his nightly rounds at Quarry End and collected the remedies he'd require.

'I pray you'll find things a little improved down there, Pa.'

'Thanks, Kezzie. You're a good lass.'

He smiled around at her as she helped him on with his heavy coat. 'Truth to tell, I'm hoping I'll not be needed for the whole of this night. You never know what happens though, so don't wait on me.'

'Very well, Pa. Here, put on your gloves. It's a cold night.'

Standing on the threshold of the apothecary, they spotted Samuel and his friends emerging noisily from the Rose and Crown across the square. Keziah could bide silent no longer.

'You're too soft with him, Pa!'

'Mebbe you're a mite too hard,' murmured Elijah, patting her shoulder. 'You think on it, eh?'

6

'Good afternoon to you, sir!'

Elijah Sephton's cheery voice drifted from the apothecary through into Meggan's parlour, where Keziah was stirring the fire and turning up the lamp in readiness for Benedict Clay's visit with her grandmother.

'It's grand seeing you again, Mr Clay — Oh, that's very kind of you! I'm right partial to a good pipe after supper. Best part of the day!

'Come through, won't you?' Elijah went on, leading the way along the hall. 'I can't join you yet awhile because I'm needed in the shop, but I'll see you later at tea. Ah, here's Keziah — ' He turned back toward the apothecary as she emerged from the parlour. 'Thanks again for the baccy, Mr Clay!'

'Miss Keziah.' Benedict Clay beamed down at her, offering a slender spray of delicate spring flowers. 'I would they were more abundant, however I found flowers in short supply.'

'They're beautiful!' she exclaimed, inclining her face to the cool, sweet fragrance of the blooms. 'I'm amazed you were able to find flowers at all so early in the year — This is harsh country, Mr Clay. Spring comes late!'

'I've noticed!' he laughed as she made to take his thick cloak and scarf. Reaching into the pocket, Clay withdrew a small cone of striped paper. 'For your young sister, if she's allowed candy — sweetmeats, I should say.'

'Oh, Edith is indeed allowed!' smiled Keziah, taking the twist of barley sugar lumps. 'Not that she has them very often. Thank you for these, Mr Clay. It'll be nice for Edith to have such a treat.

'Granny's waiting for you,' she went on, showing him into the comfortable parlour where Meggan was seated at the hearth. Between the two fireside chairs, Keziah had set the little round burr walnut table and placed upon it the lamp, the map Benedict Clay had given her, and the various bits and bobs and family treasures Meggan had brought with her from Lancashire so many years ago. Much to her regret and sorrow, Meggan's precious Book of Hours still had not been found. 'Granny, this is Mr Clay from Charleston in South Carolina.'

'I'm very pleased to meet you, ma'am.' He took her thin hand gently and bowed graciously, offering a pretty little box of chocolates. 'I've been looking forward to talking with you.'

'My word, thank you — I'm very fond of violet crèmes!' she exclaimed in delight, her bright eyes searching Benedict Clay's lean, tanned features lest they stir a recollection of somebody from home. 'Settle yourself down there by the fire, and tell me all about yourself. It was your grandfather, I believe, who left Monks Quay for America . . . ?'

Keziah left them to their discourse,

and taking her sewing up to her room, got on with replacing a button on Elijah's best Sunday shirt before collecting Edith from her lessons at the rectory and putting the finishing touches to the afternoon tea she'd prepared for Benedict Clay's visit. For once, Samuel had actually fulfilled his promise to tend the shop for the remainder of the day, so Elijah was able to join Meggan, Benedict Clay, Keziah and Edith around the tea table.

It was a lively occasion with many humorous anecdotes and observations. The American was charming and eloquent company, contributing to the amiable conversation and listening with great interest to everything everyone else had to say. Despite the absence of the Book of Hours and the family history it contained, Benedict and Meggan's deliberations had proved fruitful and there seemed considerable possibility their families were indeed related.

The American was persuaded to stay beyond afternoon tea into the early evening, however it wasn't until some while after the apothecary closed and Keziah was showing Clay out through the dark, silent shop that they were alone and she had an opportunity to ask curiously: 'How did you know Pa's favourite tobacco? Or that Granny likes violet crèmes?'

Clay laughed softly. 'I can't take any credit for the violet crèmes! I merely explained to the clerk at the confectioner's that I was seeking a gift for an elderly lady and asked his recommendation. The same with Edith's candy. As for your father's tobacco, well I recalled the sort you bought that day we were in the store together.'

She laughed too. 'I'm impressed! It was a very thoughtful gesture. And Granny's had a wonderful day. I haven't seen her so bright and animated in a long while. She's thoroughly enjoyed meeting you and talking to you.'

'The enjoyment has been mutual, I

assure you,' he replied earnestly, meeting her eyes. 'Your grandmother and your entire family have given me a connection with my past — a sense of belonging I haven't experienced for far too many years. It's a feeling I never want to lose again, Keziah.'

She caught her breath, suddenly keenly aware of his dark eyes gazing down into hers, and of Benedict's nearness as they stood together in the dim quietude of the apothecary. 'What — what will you do now?' she murmured. 'You'll be returning home, I suppose.'

'Home.' He spoke the word slowly, as though assessing its worth. 'In due course, I'll return to Charleston. As you're aware, I haven't had a real home there or anyplace else since I was a boy. Spending a while with you and your family today has made me feel the more keenly everything I've lost, and all I'm missing in my life.

'Unfortunately, I have need to return to Liverpool,' continued Clay after a moment. 'I have important business to conclude there before rejoining my ship and sailing for Charleston.'

Keziah's throat was suddenly dry. 'I wish you well in your endeavours, Mr Clay,' she added, her eyes lowered. 'And Godspeed for your travels, of course.'

'I won't be going anywhere for a while yet,' he responded quietly. 'I'm not in any hurry to leave Barrowby, Keziah.'

She swallowed hard, her pulse racing as Benedict Clay gently took her hand in his and raised it to his lips.

When he'd gone, Keziah stood alone in the darkness, her fingertips tracing his kiss, feeling over again the warm touch of Benedict's lips against her skin. Drawing in a steadying breath, she slowly locked and secured the apothecary door before turning back into the house, an unfamiliar excitement kindling deep within her.

7

She'd had a sleepless night.

It was the early morning of rent and banking day. Within very few hours, her father would be expecting Keziah to deposit the shop's takings into their account at Messrs Browning and Phipps of Caxton Street as customary. The landlord would be expecting her to call at his office and pay the rent due upon their home and the apothecary's premises. Keziah would not be able to do either, for Samuel still had not repaid the money he'd stolen from the cash-box.

Hour after hour during the long night, Keziah had lain staring at the ceiling of her room, listening to the long-case clock at the foot of the stairs striking away the endless hours of night. Wide awake yet weary to the bone, she was wearier still in mind. The dread of falling into arrears with their landlord and of not having sufficient funds to honour their other debts did not allow her any rest.

An almost greater anxiety was how she could break the news to Pa. None of this was her fault, yet Keziah knew she'd let Elijah down — deceived him and betrayed his trust. Her father would be angry, but far worse than his wrath would be his pain and disappointment at his son and daughter's duplicity.

Keziah tossed and turned in her narrow bed, fretting upon what actions might be taken by their landlord and other creditors when it became known the family could not pay what it owed. Would bailiffs be brought in? They'd lose their home, every stick and stone of it. The landlord had a reputation as a particularly litigious individual. What if he decided to prosecute Pa, and make a public example of him?

It knocked Keziah sick to think of her poor, gentle father being shamed and humiliated before a court of law. Debtors were put into prison, weren't they? Their families torn apart and left homeless . . . Round and round and round the thoughts churned inside her mind until Keziah could bear it no longer; her head would explode if she didn't rise and busy herself with chores. Any chores. Anything at all to occupy her until morning came and she could finally face up to what surely lay ahead.

Although it would be hours yet before the family was awake and about, Keziah lit the fires and fetched the water from the pump. Moving softly about the tall old house, she set the kettle to boil, mixed a batch of bread dough and put the breakfast porridge to slowly cook. As soon as the kitchen fire was burning brightly, she stood the flat irons to heat and sorted yesterday's laundry ready for pressing.

While working didn't exactly ease her agitated mind nor soothe the hollow ache in the pit of her stomach, at least Keziah was doing something instead of lying abed mithering, and she felt the better for it.

She was pressing Edith's new calico pinafore, and although she hadn't heard the yard door, Keziah felt the cold rush of draught from along the hallway as the door was silently opened. It closed equally noiselessly.

Spinning around in alarm, the flat iron still in her hand, she glimpsed Samuel sidling along towards the staircase.

'Where have you been?' she demanded in astonishment. 'I thought you were upstairs asleep!'

'Clearly, you were wrong!' He grinned lopsidedly and paused in the kitchen doorway, one shoulder propped against the jamb. 'For once in your perfectly ordered life, you were wrong.'

'You've been out all night!' charged Keziah in disgust, taking in his rumpled clothing and disheveled appearance. 'You smell like Hepworth's brewery!'

'Ah, there's a very good reason for that.' He wagged a salutary finger at

151

her. 'I'm drunk, Kez. Drunk as a lord. Have been for hours, probably.'

Keziah's patience and temper snapped. 'You're nothing short of a disgrace, Samuel! You sneak from the house and spend the night heaven knows where with your idle, drunken friends and then breeze in at this hour so intoxicated you can barely stand straight!

'You're a thief and a liar, Samuel — Haven't you an ounce of shame?'

In a couple of strides, he crossed the kitchen flags and towered over her. Snatching a purse from the pocket of his great coat, Samuel flung it across the table where she'd been ironing.

Shocked by the vehemence of the gesture, Keziah involuntarily took a step backwards, staring mutely up at him. Samuel's smooth young face was twisted with rage. She saw an unexpected flash of menace in his overly bright eyes and for a moment feared he might strike her.

That moment was fleeting, the threat

dissipating from her young brother's expression as swiftly as it appeared. His lips were curling into a sneer as he indicated the shining coins spilled amongst the garments on the table.

'Every penny, Keziah.' His voice was low, thick with alcohol and quite devoid of emotion. 'Every penny. This is over and done. I never want to hear another word from you. Do you understand?'

Keziah ignored him, gathering up the coins and replacing them into the purse. 'I'll take your word the full amount owed is here. Where did you get it?'

'Don't *dare* interrogate me, Kez!' he spat contemptuously. 'You wanted the money, and you've got the money. Never satisfied, that's your trouble. That, and being so damned sanctimonious!'

'I'll not be party to any more of your deceptions,' she said levelly. 'Have you come by this money honestly, Samuel?'

'It's none of your business,' he

murmured, a sly grin suddenly spreading across his flushed face. 'If you must know, I won it!'

'*Won it?*' she repeated in consternation. 'There's a lot of money here. Where — *how* — could you possibly win such a large sum?'

He tapped the side of his nose with a forefinger and winked conspiratorially. 'Sister dear, outside this godforsaken shop there's a world of pleasure and temptation and profit beyond your wildest dreams — if you ever have wild dreams, which frankly I doubt!'

Yawning widely, Samuel sank onto one of the ladder-backed kitchen chairs and ran a palm across his face. 'I'm ready for my bed. Fetch me some tea, Kez. I'll take it up with me. A slice of that pie wouldn't go amiss, either.'

She'd bent to set the irons above the fire to heat once more and without looking at her brother, returned to the table, smoothing her hands over the seams of Edith's pinafore in readiness for pressing.

'You know where the kettle and the tea-chest are, Samuel,' commented Keziah at length. 'If you want victuals, you can fetch them yourself. I'll not wait upon you!'

'You forget your place here!' His lethargy vanished in an instant and Samuel was on his feet, scraping back the chair with such force it crashed to the stone flags.

Using the dresser to steady himself, he lurched towards the door, glowering over his shoulder at her.

'Don't cross me, Keziah — or I'll make you sorrier than you'd ever imagine!'

8

'You're looking right peaky this morning, lass,' remarked Elijah several hours later, considering Keziah's drawn face as they worked together in the dispensary. 'Are you not feeling too good?'

'I'm fine, Pa,' she replied mechanically, turning to smile up at him. Samuel's anger and the violence of his parting threat earlier that morning had badly shaken her.

Even now, with Samuel safely upstairs and sleeping it off in his room, she felt unnerved. Keziah's hands were trembling slightly as she measured ingredients and poured the medicinal mixtures into bottles. Her countenance was ashen, making the smudges of shadow beneath her eyes appear even darker.

'I'm a bit tired, that's all,' she said, adding truthfully, 'I didn't get much sleep last night.'

'Our Samuel's the exact opposite!' said her father cheerfully, selecting roots of dandelion from the drawer. 'He must be sleeping like a log. The lad turned in straight after supper last night, and he's not stirred his stumps yet!'

Keziah said nothing, her brow knitted. The more she thought upon her brother's erratic behaviour, the more disturbing she found it. For all his various faults, bouts of vile temper and violence were certainly not Samuel's nature. It had to have been the liquor's malign influence upon him, and *that* scared Keziah more than anything. Her brother was an intelligent and well-educated young man; how could he be weak and foolish enough to allow alcohol to take control of his very senses?

'Samuel knows I go to the bank and pay the landlord today,' she remarked, her gaze intent upon her work. 'He should be here helping you. It's too bad of him, Pa.'

'He's still a growing lad who needs his sleep,' responded Elijah mildly. 'Besides, Samuel's pulled his weight grand this past week with not so much as a grumble or long face. Him having a few hours' extra sleep won't hurt anybody and if needs be, I'll manage alright on my own while you're out — Hello, pet!' he broke off as Edith ran through the arch from the house and cannoned around the corner into the dispensary. 'My, don't you look the bobby-dazzler? Is that pinny new?'

'Kezzie just finished making it for me!' She nodded, turning all about to show off the new garment. 'Look, Pa. It has flowers and my name in fancy stitches on the pocket!'

'By gum, so it has! Your sister's always been handy with a needle and thread. Do you reckon she'll make me one of them, so I can wear it here in the shop?'

Edith giggled, flouncing out the pleat in the pinafore. 'When I come home, Kezzie's showing me how to make seedy cakes. We're going to make lots and lots, aren't we?'

'We'd better, young lady — 'else there'll be nothing sweet for folk to eat at the church social!' remarked Keziah, fetching Edith's bonnet and coat from the hall. 'We'd best be off now, or I'll have Mrs Kennard after me for keeping you late for lessons!'

★   ★   ★

Putting on her own bonnet and cloak, Keziah took the pouch of money from the desk drawer and stowed it safely into the depths of her bag, fastening it securely to her waist before following her young sister through the shop. Edith wrapped both hands around the handle and pulled open the heavy door, setting the brass bell jangling vigorously and almost colliding with the man about to enter.

'George!' she shrieked in delight, looking back over her shoulder to where Keziah was straightening her bonnet in the reflection on one of the glass-fronted cupboards. 'Kezzie, it's George come to take us in the waggon!'

'George.' Keziah froze where she stood. They hadn't seen nor spoken to each other since the encounter outside Pearce's tea-room. 'I hadn't expected to see you today.'

'It's bank day,' he mumbled awkwardly, framed by the doorway and turning his cap in both hands as he hesitantly met her gaze. 'I always come for you on bank day. It's not safe, a lass alone carrying all that money. I always take you.'

'Yes. Yes, you do,' she responded softly, stepping forward and closing the couple of yards separating them. 'Your thoughtfulness is greatly appreciated.'

'I don't do it for thoughtfulness, Kez,' he muttered gruffly, holding the door as she brushed past him. 'You know the reason why!'

She glanced back keenly, their eyes meeting for but a moment before Keziah turned again, catching her lip between her teeth and saying nothing as she hastened to Erskine's waggon, where Edith was standing on tiptoe stroking the pair of roan horses. She'd really missed seeing Tinker and Beauty, and missed seeing George too. He hadn't been looking in at the apothecary a couple of times each day like he usually did, nor sometimes staying for supper or taking her and Kezzie out in the waggon after church on Sundays.

Edith liked George a lot, and she made the most of the drive up through town to St Harmon's rectory by chattering nineteen to the dozen and telling him all the news he'd missed.

Once at the rectory, Edith clambered down from the waggon and ran along the path towards the front door to be greeted by the Kennards' maid — scarcely more than a child herself — who was waiting there for the pupils to arrive. Pausing on the steps, Edith turned and waved happily to her sister and George before rubbing her stout boots on the coarse jute mat and

161

disappearing into the rectory.

'Wish I'd taken to schooling like that little one,' commented George, jiggling the reins so the heavy horses plodded away from St Harmon's. 'If I had, I'd be a better man now, that's for sure!'

'You may have finished your schooling too soon,' remarked Keziah absently, gazing into the distance as they started downwards into the town. 'But you're a far better man than many who've had the soundest of education.'

He considered her sidelong, taking a pretty good guess at what notion lay behind her words but setting that aside for the time being. There was something else needed to be put right first.

'I'm sorry, Kez,' he began bluntly, 'about the other day. It was stupid. Daft. I don't know what came over me. I just saw red and . . . Anyhow, what I did was wrong. Dead wrong. And I'm sorry for it.'

'Your apology is accepted, George,' she answered quietly, her eyes holding his. 'However it's not so much what you

did that I found disappointing —
although, heaven knows, that was
humiliating enough — but rather your
obvious poor opinion of me!'

'Poor opinion?' he spluttered in
disbelief. 'No woman was ever held in
higher regard than I have for you!'

'Then you have a peculiar way of
showing it!' she maintained firmly. 'I
was in the company of someone who is
clearly not only a distinguished gentleman but also an acquaintance of my
family and quite possibly a blood
relative, yet you took exception!'

'For all his fancy talk and frills, he's a
stranger, Kez!' persisted George, vexed.
'A foreigner you know next to nowt
about, and you'd been in the tea-rooms
with him!'

'Yes, George,' she returned crisply.
'Mr Clay and I had had morning coffee
and pastries at Pearce's. A more proper
and civilised activity would be difficult
to conceive, however you chose to make
an exhibition of yourself and embarrass
Mr Clay and myself by bawling my

name in the street — '

'Enough, Kez! Don't go on so!' he cut in, scowling at her. 'That first time he came to the apothecary, I saw the way he looked at you — Lord above, I'd have had to be blind not to!'

'This is absurd!' she exclaimed impatiently, fussing with her gloves. 'I can't believe I'm hearing such non-sense!'

Turning the waggon into the mews alongside Millersgate, George brought the horses to a halt and turned to face her squarely.

'Can it be you really don't under-stand, or are you twisting the knife to keep me in the wrong?' he challenged bitterly. 'I was jealous, Keziah! Aye, so jealous my blood was up and pounding in my veins. When I saw you coming out of Pearce's with him — saw him taking your arm like he had the right to do it, and the pair of you go walking off — all I wanted was to knock him flat!'

George looked away, expelling a ragged breath before continuing more steadily. 'I can't hold a candle to the likes of him, Kez. I'm not of his class, and I'm not so daft I don't know it.'

Keziah sat motionless, at a loss what to say.

'You have absolutely no cause to — for concern,' she finally replied, staring ahead to the crush of traffic weaving at snail's pace up along the main street. 'Mr Clay is charming and polite, as I believe is merely his custom. He has visited Granny and taken tea with our family. Benedict Clay is my *friend*, George.

'Why don't we forget the incident at Pearce's occurred?' Keziah suggested quietly. 'Can we not allow things to be as they were?'

George earnestly searched her face before nodding, his own face relaxing into a grin. 'Aye, that'd suit me grand!'

'Me too,' she smiled, adding, 'It's very considerate of you, accompanying me to the bank.'

'What else was I to do?' He shrugged, reaching for her gloved hand and holding it briefly before taking up the reins and starting from the mews. 'I may not be a gentleman, but I'd not put any woman at risk from falling prey to robbers.'

'You're more of a true gentleman than anybody I know, George Cunliffe!' she said stoutly, reflecting soberly, 'Actually, the apothecary's banking is an errand I had not believed would be possible today. Nor was paying our rent to the landlord!'

'It's that blasted Samuel again, isn't it?' he demanded in exasperation. 'Soon as I saw you, I knew there was summat troubling you! What's he been up to now?'

Keziah stared at George unhappily. In the brief while since they'd fallen out over Benedict Clay, she'd missed him terribly. There'd been emptiness in her days that no amount of keeping busy had been able to fill. She'd longed to simply be with him; to share his company and talk to him; seek his thoughts and advice.

Now, as George urged her confidence, Keziah's pent-up anxieties spilled over.

' . . . Samuel's drinking too much and his behaviour is wild and wilful,' she concluded dismally. 'Often-times, he doesn't seem himself at all. This morning there was a — a *fury* — in his eyes that, well — It frightened me!'

George swore softly under his breath. 'That lad needs a good hiding to knock some sense into him. If he ever raises his hand to you, Kez, he'll have *me* to reckon with!'

'I'm sure he would never really do such a thing,' she insisted hastily. 'Can it actually be true Samuel won such a large sum gambling?'

George snorted derisively. 'Fortunes have been gained or lost on the turn of a wager, Kez! No doubt about that. Happen Samuel got lucky and won the money fair and square, like he told you.

'But if he's dealing fast and loose with the likes of his Castlehill pals and their rich cronies, then the lad's even dafter than I thought!' concluded

George grimly. 'It's fine while he's winning, but what's going to happen when Samuel loses and can't pay up? Their sort may have money to burn, but they'll show no mercy if he welshes on a bet!'

Keziah paled, running her tongue over dry lips. 'Do you know anything, George? About where Samuel goes by night, and whatever he's become involved with?'

'No, but I've eyes and ears and I know this town well enough. Samuel may have been thick with the Baldwin brothers and Reggie Crane since schooldays, but they're a feckless bunch who think they can get away with murder in Barrowby — and since their families are the town's gentry, they likely could!

'Samuel's playing with fire, Kez. If he crosses any one of them, mark my words, they'll close ranks and cut him down without a second thought! The lad won't know what's hit him. He'll be finished.'

'Whatever can I do?' breathed Keziah desperately. 'Samuel obviously can't see the dangers for himself, so *I'll* have to do something!'

'What, exactly?' reasoned George shortly, turning onto Caxton Street. 'Face it, Kez. He's a grown man and it's high time you were done with bandaging his knees and sending him back out to play without a care in the world!'

'But — '

'You can scold him and mollycoddle him till you're blue in the face, but Samuel'll go his own sweet way and there's nowt you can do to stop him!'

'He's young still — Pa's right about that,' she protested. 'Samuel's naïve for his age, too. I can't abandon him to his fate. He's my brother, George! It's my duty to care for him. I am his elder sister, after all!'

'I'm sorry, lass,' continued George more gently. 'This isn't what you want to hear, but Samuel *isn't* your responsibility any more. You can't go on protecting him forever. A man has to make his own choices in this life — and his own mistakes.'

Keziah averted her eyes. Although every word George said was sensible . . .

'Whatever Samuel does,' she murmured at length, 'I could never turn my back on him.'

George sighed heavily. 'No, I don't expect you can. If you did, you wouldn't be you . . . Shall we be going to that social at St Harmon's then?'

'Oh, yes!' she responded, adding tentatively, 'If that's agreeable to you?'

''Course it is! I'll call for you.' He grinned, drawing up outside Browning and Phipps. 'After the shop closes?'

'Perfect! Mr Kennard asked the womenfolk to bake, so I'll be taking a crock of seedy cakes and plumbread.' She glanced toward the gleaming brass and polished oak doors of the bank. 'I'd best get on. Thank you, George. For bringing me here.'

'It's my pleasure, Kez.' Had they not

been in a busy street, George would have been tempted to steal a kiss, but had to make do with squeezing Keziah's gloved hand before helping her down from the waggon and escorting her up the marble steps and into the imposing entrance of Browning and Phipps.

'I'll be at Erskine's yard all morning, then I'm off over to Hawbeck with a delivery. I'll look in at the apothecary on the way. You could come with me, if you like?' he went on hopefully. 'If you can get away for the afternoon.'

'I can't — but an outing would've been most enjoyable!' she responded ruefully. 'It's quite a distance to Hawbeck. I'll pack you a snap-tin for the journey and see you before you set off.'

* * *

With the apothecary's takings safely deposited, Keziah made her way from Caxton Street and across town to the

171

cramped premises of the Sephtons' landlord in Fletcher Street. She had her hand upon the door and was about to enter when, from the corner of her eye, Keziah spotted a young girl she recognised waving and hurrying towards her.

'Betsy!' she exclaimed. 'I haven't seen you in such a while! How are you?'

'Well enough, Miss Sephton, thank you for asking,' replied Betsy Sharples, catching her breath. 'I only get half a day off a month now I'm skivvying for the nobs, so I don't get down into town much anymore. I wouldn't be here today only I'm doing messages for Cook. Did you know I'd left the laundry?'

'Your mother told me you'd got a place in one of the big houses at Castlehill,' nodded Keziah, as they moved a little away from the landlord's doorway to permit a downtrodden-looking clerk to enter. 'Do you like working up there? It must be quite different from the laundry!'

'You can say that again! And aye, I like it well enough.' Betsy shrugged, wrinkling her nose. 'It's no bed of roses, though. With the laundry, once you'd knocked off you could go home and do what you liked till the next day. At Castlehill, it's all rules! You can't do this and you can't do that and you have to go to church every Sunday with the rest of the household.

'You're never really finished, neither,' she added with a shake of her bright copper ringlets. 'We're at their beck and call morning, noon and night. Still, can't have everything, can you?'

'Living-in must be difficult,' sympathised Keziah thoughtfully. 'I don't know how I'd cope. I'd miss my family too much.'

'Hrumph! My family's the reason why I went into service! Mam and Da already had a houseful of bairns, then our Flo got wed and her and Norman moved in with us. She's always in the family way, our Flo. I was fed up sleeping head-to-tail with brothers and sisters and nieces and nephews!' explained Betsy with a grin that lit up her plump, pretty face. 'At least at Castlehill, I've a bed all to myself, get to wear clean clothes and have three decent meals every day! Can you blame me for leaving home?'

'Not when you put it like that!' laughed Keziah. 'My mother and grandmother were both in service so I've some idea how hard and demanding the work is. Nevertheless, it must be pleasant living in such beautiful surroundings. The houses at Castlehill look so light and airy with those huge shining windows, and the gardens are a joy to behold.'

'It's a different world than down here in the town, that's for sure,' remarked Betsy sagely. 'It's a grand house and the Baldwins are — '

'Your employers are the *Baldwins?*' queried Keziah with a surprised smile. 'Why, Samuel knows their sons! They were school friends in York.'

'Aye, I know. I see him there

174

often — ' She broke off, going on hurriedly, 'From a distance, you understand! I'm not allowed above stairs when the family and visitors are about. Mind you, I never see much of the Baldwin brothers and their pals anyway. Nor talk to them, of course. It wouldn't be proper.'

'Samuel was recently invited to a musical evening at the Baldwins' home,' began Keziah with a widening smile. 'When he came back afterwards, I was eager to know what everything looked like! I wanted to hear about the furniture and the ladies' gowns and jewels and finery and suchlike, but you know what Samuel's like — He hadn't noticed a single thing except the music!'

Betsy nodded, her cheeks pink. 'That night, I managed to hide outside the French windows so I could hear him play. The music wasn't really sad, but it made me want to cry — Isn't that queer?'

Keziah shook her head. 'Music

touches the soul, Betsy. That you were moved by it is a fine compliment to Samuel's playing. I'm sure he was extremely flattered.'

'Oh, I didn't tell him — I couldn't!' she exclaimed, adding with a sigh, 'Samuel's always been . . . *special!* I love listening to him talk about the places he wants to go and the things he plans on doing! He's not like the rest of the lads in this miserable old town, Miss Sephton. Samuel is really going to *be* somebody one day. Make his mark, if you know what I mean?'

'Let's hope you're right!' remarked Keziah drily.

'I'm keen to make good too, such as I can,' declared Betsy with a determined bob of her head. 'First step was getting out of Skinner Street and up to Castlehill amongst the quality. I don't want to be in service forever, mind.

'There's a parlour maid at the Baldwins'. Must be thirty if she's a day and she's *still* there, polishing furniture and lighting fires. Will be the rest of her life, I suppose, for she's too old to wed now,' opined Betsy dispassionately. 'I don't want to end up like her, Miss Sephton! I mean to better myself. Does that sound daft, coming from the likes of me?'

'Certainly not, Betsy,' replied Keziah, her expression gentle as she considered the earnest young woman standing before her. 'You're determined and sensible, and you work hard.

'After Granny had her fall, you were the greatest help to our family when you came in and lent a hand at the apothecary. You read and write well, and figure accurately. Those are very useful skills, Betsy, and you have a polite, pleasing manner with customers, too. I know Pa will provide an excellent character reference, if ever you wished to apply for a position in a shop.'

'Would he really?' exclaimed Betsy in surprise. 'Oh, I'd *like* to work in a shop! That'd be a real step up the ladder. Summat to be proud of. At a dressmaker's establishment, maybe?

Somewhere clean and genteel,' she giggled suddenly, her small ungloved hand flying to her full pink lips. 'Knowing my luck, I'd end up in the ironmonger's — lugging coal scuttles and buckets of nails!'

They both laughed, and Keziah asked, 'If you've time, won't you come back and have a cup of tea? I know Gran would be delighted to see you again!'

'That's right nice of you, Miss Sephton,' replied Betsy, pleased by the unexpected invitation. 'I'd like that. I truly would. But Cook'll have it in for me summat shocking if I don't get back soon with her messages.'

'Another time perhaps,' replied Keziah warmly, adding with a mischievous smile, 'But if you happen to be near the apothecary today, you may just find Samuel behind the counter — although I have to warn you, when I left the house this morning he was still sound asleep!'

'Had a late night, I expect,' replied

Betsy matter-of-factly, adding in a flurry of explanation, 'That is, I mean, I happened to see Samuel at Castlehill last evening. With the Baldwin brothers and Reggie Crane. They all went out together, so I just thought . . . '

'I daresay you're right,' replied Keziah cheerfully, deliberately keeping her tone light. 'Young men do appear to lose all track of time when they're off on their jaunts!'

'That they do!' agreed Betsy eagerly. 'I happen to know — from the maid who does the beds at Castlehill — that the Baldwin brothers' beds weren't slept in last night! Those naughty boys weren't home for breakfast, neither!'

The two women chatted a little while longer before going their separate ways, however as Keziah entered the land-lord's office to pay her family's rent, there were many more questions and apprehensions about Samuel's secretive activities coursing through her mind.

★ ★ ★

She was returning along Caxton Street, glancing into shop windows without really paying much attention to their contents, when something in Stephenson's window caught Keziah's eye. It was tucked away in the far corner, but directly in her line of vision as she approached the dusty little stationer's.

Keziah froze, staring at a small, dog-eared book propped amongst a display of well-worn novels and other second-hand books. Moving a pace or two closer, she bent forward, peering through the grimy glass pane to gain a better look. Surely it couldn't be —

Keziah recognised the book at once! There could be none other quite like it in Barrowby.

This *was* Gran's treasured Book of Hours!

9

Herbert Stephenson, the proprietor, was away at an auction in Ripon, so after a brief and fruitless conversation with the bookseller's callow assistant, Keziah sped homewards.

Resisting the impulse to burst into the apothecary and confront her brother, she went through the yard and in at the back door, not waiting to take off her bonnet and cloak before sweeping into the shop. Elijah was attending to a customer at the counter so Samuel was alone in the dispensary.

'I want to talk to you!' she demanded in a low voice. 'Privately.'

'Can't it wait?' Samuel replied lazily, turning his back. 'I'm busy.'

Keziah bridled. 'I'd like your opinion upon something I've lately seen in Caxton Street.'

She fancied she saw a tension about

Samuel's shoulders, but still he didn't turn around and face her.

'You've sold Gran's book to Stephenson's, haven't you?'

Samuel glanced sidelong, staring at her insolently. 'Stephenson's?'

'The stationer and bookseller in Caxton Street!' she retorted angrily. 'I've *seen* Gran's book in the shop window!'

'I haven't the slightest idea what you're talking about,' he answered coolly. 'Would you mind leaving me to my work?'

'Enough of your lies!' She stepped around the bench, keeping her voice low so Elijah could not overhear. 'There's no time to be lost, Samuel. We have to buy that book back!'

'Buy it with what exactly?' he sneered. 'That old book of Gran's barely raised sufficient for a decent wager at the card-table! And since repaying a certain little sum to you this morning, I've scarcely any winnings left!'

Rage and frustration erupted within Keziah. She wanted to lash out — *force* him to help her recover Gran's book . . . But her passion was futile. She couldn't compel Samuel to do anything. Keziah was utterly powerless. And knew it only too well.

'The Book of Hours means everything to our grandmother,' she appealed, clenching her fingers into her palms and keeping her temper. 'Since it went missing, Gran's constantly searching for it. Selfish as you are, even *you* must realise how deeply troubled she is! Come with me to Stephenson's, Samuel — Somehow, we *must* find a way of retrieving that book, or Gran will never know another moment's peace of mind — '

'You're overwrought and you're exaggerating,' he remarked wearily, selecting jars of comfrey, thyme and liquorice root from the shelves and setting them out upon the bench. 'Gran's an old woman. She forgets things. In another week, she won't even remember the blasted book ever existed.'

'That's a cruel and wicked thing to say!' hissed Keziah, glancing across to where Elijah was still engaged with the customer. 'To have stolen something from her is despicable, but allowing Gran to continue searching and suffering the torment of doubting her wits and fearing she's losing her mind is beneath contempt!'

'I deny everything,' he responded evenly, blending ingredients with the heavy marble pestle.

'You should be ashamed of yourself!' she retorted in disgust. 'Not only a common thief, but too much the coward to face Gran and own up to what you've done!'

'You're holier-than-thou for both of us, Keziah,' he remarked with a bored sigh, adding, 'By the by, I'm not in the least concerned you'll run tattle-tale to Grandmother and Pa. We both know you won't do that — Don't we?'

Keziah spun on her heel, quitting the dispensary but pausing at the arch, her hand upon the wall. Her heart was hammering in her chest and hot, hopeless tears were prickling behind her eyes.

'Hello, lass!' Elijah looked around from the counter as his customer departed. 'Everything go alright at the bank and such?'

'Hmm? Oh, yes! Yes. All done, Pa,' she managed with a nod, not meeting his eyes. 'I need to go out again though. Shouldn't be long. There's something I must do . . .'

After looking in on Meggan, who was sorting through the ragbag of cloth bits for suitable pieces to replace two worn patches in Edith's quilt, and ensuring her grandmother didn't need anything, Keziah sped away from the apothecary.

Walking as quickly as she was able without actually breaking into a run, she weaved through a maze of narrow, twisting ginnels and crossed town by the shortest route to Canning Place. George wasn't due to leave for Hawbeck until after noon, and Keziah was praying he hadn't departed earlier than anticipated and was still in his cubby-hole of an office above Erskine's stable yard.

Hitching up her skirts, she darted over the cobbles and clambered up the steep stone steps running up the outside of the stable's wall to the loft.

'Thank goodness you're still here!' she exclaimed breathlessly, her face scarlet and moist with perspiration as she burst into the small room where George was seated at a rough table, scratching away at a writing tablet with a pen sorely in need of trimming. 'I was afraid you'd be gone!'

'I'll be a while yet setting off for Hawbeck — What's wrong?' George was on his feet and around the table at once. 'Is it your gran?'

She shook her head, gulping in a deep breath and gabbling about seeing Meggan's book and confronting Samuel.

' ... I don't know what to do, George!' she concluded rapidly, colour draining from her damp face. 'Once the book is sold, Gran will never —

'What are you doing?'

'Taking some money with us,' he answered, counting a tidy sum from a cupboard hidden away in the corner of the loft and writing a few words upon a scrap of paper before replacing the tin and locking the cupboard. 'We'll need it.

'Stephenson's bought the book from Samuel fair and square, Kez. They're not going to hand it back to us without turning a profit,' George commented, going ahead of her out onto the stone steps and guiding her down past the loaded waggon towards the street. 'Hitching the horses will waste too much time. Besides, the traffic going up to Caxton Street'll be heavy at this hour. We'll be quicker on foot!'

Cutting through the ginnels and courts, they emerged onto Caxton Street a short distance from the stationer's premises. A few yards closer, and Keziah's spirits plummeted. The book was gone from the window display.

'Don't lose hope — We're not beaten yet!' muttered George, pushing open the stiff door and striding up to the counter.

'Good morning,' he began, when the pasty-faced young clerk stepped forward. 'You had an old prayer book — '

'I've already explained to the lady, sir,' interrupted the youth, cautiously eyeing George Cunliffe's muscular frame. 'It was Mr Stephenson himself purchased the book and he's away to Ripon. I know nothing about — '

★ ★ ★

'The book's gone from the window!' blurted Keziah, unable to contain her impatience. 'Are we too late? Surely it cannot have been sold already!'

The clerk cleared his throat, running a thin finger around the front of his stiff collar. 'I'm afraid so, madam. Purchased by one of our regular customers

— a most respectable elderly gentleman. A former master at the grammar school, actually,' concluded the young man, casting a nervous glance in George's direction. 'I'm only Mr Stephenson's clerk, sir. I wasn't even here when that book was brought into the shop! My word 'pon it, I don't know anything about it. It was for sale and I sold it. That's all, sir. I'm sorry.'

'You're not at fault in any way,' George reassured calmly. 'It's our mistake the book fetched up here in your shop. A simple mistake, so we want to buy it back.'

'You said one of your regular customers purchased it?' persisted Keziah, clinging to the slim hope all might not yet be lost. 'Then you will know the gentleman's name and address?'

'Well, yes, of course, but — '

'We only want to make him an offer to buy back the book,' put in George, fixing the younger man's gaze. 'We're not after causing any trouble —

'*His name, sir!*'

'This is most irregular. I'm not sure Mr Stephenson would approve,' blustered the clerk uncomfortably, his eyes darting beyond them to the doorway, where a lady and gentlemen with three young sons were entering. 'Look, you must excuse me! I've customers to attend to.'

'You have us to attend to first, lad,' George insisted firmly, setting his hand onto the counter, palm down, and pushing coins barely concealed beneath it towards the young man. 'Like I said, we want no trouble. Give us the gentleman's name and address and we'll leave you to your business. No one'll ever know you've told us, and you'd be doing us a great favour.'

'Please help us!' implored Keziah, her fingertips gripping the edge of the counter. 'The book means so very much to my family!'

The young man eyed the coins, while

Keziah held her breath and the lady and gentleman grew ever more impatient for service.

'I suppose with it being a matter of such personal importance to you . . . Mister Joshua Bell from Keepers Ford,' murmured the clerk, his thin lips barely moving as his gaze slid from Keziah to the prosperous family while his hand moved almost imperceptibly across the counter, palming the coins. 'Good morning, Mr Moore! Mrs Moore. How may I assist you today . . . ?'

Slipping from the musty dimness into the cold brightness of the March morning, Keziah was weak with relief.

'Oh, well done, George! I didn't think he was going to tell us the man's name!'

'We were lucky there was wealthy folk waiting to be served — and we were dealing with the clerk and not his boss! Stephenson himself mightn't have been so ready to oblige about a regular customer, 'specially not a gentleman and scholar,' opined George shrewdly.

'Whereas a young and poorly paid lad like yon youth was glad of t'brass and could see no harm telling us what we wanted to know.'

'Keepers Ford,' reflected Keziah. 'That's a considerable distance away beyond the castle, isn't it? Can we go there straight away?'

''fraid not.' George shook his head. 'I have to get back to Erskine's, for I've that delivery to Hawbeck to make today. Besides, being a man of quality, this Mr Bell wouldn't see us if we just show up on his doorstone.

'No, we need to do this proper, Kez. We'll have to ask Mr Bell if we can call on him. Let him know why we want to talk to him,' went on George thoughtfully, his mind turning over possibilities. 'You go on home and write him a letter. Make it plain we accept he owns the book now, but explain about your gran and ask if we can call on him — ' George broke off, his forehead creasing into a deep frown. 'But it'll have to be tomorrow when we go. Ask if we can call on him tomorrow morning.'

'Tomorrow?' she echoed in dismay, anxious to set about recovering the Book of Hours immediately. 'Can we not go this evening, after you return from Hawbeck?'

'I'm already late setting off, Kez! I'll likely not get back this side of midnight as it is,' countered George practically. 'Anyhow, we can't do owt until you've written to Mr Bell and he's sent his reply.'

'What if Mr Bell *doesn't* reply?' she fretted, catching her lip between her teeth. 'Or if he refuses to receive us? Oh, George — Whatever will we do then?'

'Cross that bridge when we come to it!' replied George firmly, quickening his pace as they walked. 'I'll get this job for Erskine done, then first thing tomorrow morning I'll get spruced up in my Sunday best and we'll drive out to Keepers Ford.'

At the corner of Canning Place, they paused.

'Seems to me, our only hope is Mr Bell taking pity on your story and letting us buy the book off him,' George commented. 'I *can* borrow a bit o'brass from Erskine's, but we still mightn't be able to afford it.

'I'm sorry, Kez,' he concluded apologetically. 'It may be your gran's book is gone for good.'

10

Several hours later, Keziah came down-stairs with the bundle of newly purchased flannelette and could've wept. Her grand-mother was painstakingly turning out cupboards and drawers for the ump-teenth time, convinced the Book of Hours must be somewhere within the house and she had but to search thoroughly to find it.

'Gran, could you give me a hand?' began Keziah shakily, making much of unfolding the flannelette and spreading it out across the table. 'While — while I'm not needed in the shop is a good chance to start cutting out the night-gowns.'

'Aye, hang on,' replied Meggan, carefully replacing the contents of the dresser drawer before joining Keziah at the table. 'I'll hold onto this end, shall I?'

'Please. I'll trim off these frayed bits first.' Straightening the edges of the flannelette, Keziah took up the shears. 'There! Now, if you'll keep it taut . . . '

Thus the afternoon wore on, with Keziah constantly listening for a call through from the shop that a boy was come with a message for her. She'd composed several drafts of the letter to Mr Bell before deciding upon the final, polite and courteous request she hoped with all her heart the learned gentleman would not decline. She'd entrusted the letter with the boy from the Rose and Crown inn, who was a sensible lad, and instructed him to await a reply — if there was one.

The boy hadn't yet returned, however Keziah was aware he'd have other errands to complete so had no choice but patiently wait. With George gone to Hawbeck, there wasn't anything she could do before the morrow anyway.

She and Gran were seated together in the parlour, and Keziah was tacking the long seam of Edith's nightgown when

Pa looked around the doorway. 'Mr Clay's here to see you, lass — Shall I send him through?'

After pleasantries were exchanged, Benedict Clay apologised for disturbing Meggan and Keziah at their needle-work.

' . . . I can see I've called at an inopportune time. I was very much hoping you'd do me the honour of joining me for afternoon tea at the Wild Swan, Miss Keziah,' he explained amiably. 'Although I'm hardly an expert upon English afternoon tea, I'm assured by the landlady that the Wild Swan does put on an exceedingly impressive spread!'

'That's true, and your invitation is kind,' frowned Keziah, unable to think of aught else but whether Joshua Bell had received her letter and if he would agree to an interview. 'However, I'm afraid — '

'Away with you, Kezzie!' interrupted Meggan mildly. 'Afternoon tea at the Wild Swan would be a grand treat, and it'll do you the world of good! You've been looking right washed-out lately. Your pa and Samuel are in the shop, and there's nowt waiting to be done here, so what's to stop you going out for once? Nay, I'll not have any arguing — Away with the pair of you and enjoy yourselves!'

Keziah hesitated, gazing into the inviting warmth of Benedict Clay's dark eyes. A rush of hot colour infused her cheeks at recollection of their last meeting in the shadowy apothecary, and of Benedict's lips tenderly brushing her skin.

'Very well,' she got out, her heart suddenly beating faster. 'Afternoon tea would be pleasant. Thank you.'

'The thanks are entirely mine, Miss Keziah,' smiled Benedict, his eyes dancing. 'It isn't actually raining today, and I believe there's a pleasant walk along a river that runs close by the Wild Swan. If the weather continues dry, perhaps we might walk together a while? I've seen little of Barrowby and its surroundings and would like to take some memories of the town back home with me.'

'You're soon to leave us then, Mr Clay?' enquired Meggan, removing pins from the flannelette and pushing them into the well-worn velvet cushion tied about her left wrist.

'At the month's end,' he replied ruefully. 'I must rejoin my ship at Liverpool, Mrs Worsley. However, I do intend to sail back to England in the fall.

'I aim to visit Monks Quay and explore the places you've told me about — places that would have been familiar to my grandfather and his family. I may even find the little homestead where he was born and raised!'

'It's nigh on half a lifetime since I left Monks Quay,' mused Meggan incredulously. 'I doubt it's much changed, though. You don't get change in the country same as you do in a town. The changes I saw while Frank and me lived in Harrogate! Even here in Barrowby, there's been all sorts changed since I came here.

'I'd dearly like to see Monks Quay once more — though I never shall. It's too far away and I'm far too old for such a journey!' she laughed, going on, 'I'd like to meet up with my brother-in-law again, too. I've not heard from Brough in years! Mind, he never was much for letter-writing. It was my sister, Lou, who wrote regular and kept in touch.'

'If I remember rightly,' began Benedict thoughtfully, 'you said Brough and Lou lived at the beach in Greendow Cottage, where you and she — and your mother and grandmother before you — were born and raised?'

'You've a grand memory for names and places, lad!' responded Meggan, pleased. 'Aye, that's right. Greendow Cottage is our old home. A few months after Lou passed away, Brough came to Harrogate and visited Frank and me. I've not seen him since then. He'd already retired from the sea and come ashore, so I'm not sure what he'll be doing now. Seaweeding, maybe.'

Meggan talked a while longer of Monks Quay and times past, while Keziah slipped upstairs to tidy her hair and make ready for her outing with Benedict Clay. However, even as she was standing before the glass in her room, critically considering her reflection and hastily tucking stray wisps neatly beneath her bonnet, Keziah's thoughts were agitated, her mind distracted, and the knot of apprehension becoming ever more taut within her as she awaited Joshua Bell's response to her letter.

It came in the moments after she and Benedict had bidden Meggan good-bye and were on their way from the shop. Immediately they'd quit the apothecary and the heavy door closed behind them, Keziah broke the seal on the small, square letter.

'He no longer has it!' she gasped, raising despairing eyes to her companion. 'I'm too late, Benedict!'

'Excuse me?'

'I'm sorry.' She shook her head dismally, meeting Benedict's mystified gaze and accepting his arm. 'You'll think I've taken leave of my senses . . . '

Handing him Joshua Bell's letter, Keziah bleakly explained the circumstances surrounding the correspondence.

' . . . George and I had intended calling upon Mr Bell tomorrow morning,' she concluded unhappily as they were walking through town towards the river. 'However, as you see from his letter, Mr Bell no longer *has* Gran's book! There isn't any point in our visiting him.'

'I disagree, Keziah,' Benedict remarked at once, returning Joshua Bell's letter. 'But firstly — You are absolutely *certain* the prayer book Mr Bell purchased is the book belonging to your grandmother?'

'There's no doubt about that, Mr Clay,' she answered, grateful for the American's tact. She'd observed the query in his eyes, but Benedict Clay was far too gallant to question how on earth Meggan Worsley's precious family keepsake had been removed from her possession and sold to a local stationer! 'It *is* Granny's Book of Hours!'

'Forgive me if I presume too much upon our friendship, Miss Keziah,' he responded at length. 'Please do not be offended by what I'm about to suggest, but since you're sure this is the missing book, there's no time to waste before speaking with Mr Joshua Bell.'

'For what purpose?' she demanded edgily. 'He doesn't have it!'

'Isn't it therefore imperative we ascertain the book's whereabouts so we can buy it back?' Benedict paused before going on quietly, 'Whatever the sum required, allow me the honour of funding the enterprise — No, I insist, Miss Keziah! It's but a small gesture of kinship, and one that will permit me a real sense of belonging to your family. I beg you, don't reject it!'

His was a heartfelt and unassuming plea, and Keziah felt churlish about voicing the refusal on the tip of her tongue. Aware of Benedict's gaze upon her, she drew a measured breath. Keziah had been agonising about breaking the news to Meggan, if her book should be irrevocably lost . . .

Clay read Keziah's hesitation as acquiescence, and responded. 'Thank you, Keziah. I propose we set off directly to Mr Bell's home.'

'Keepers Ford is outside town at the far side of the castle ruins,' she commented vaguely, thoughts tumbling one over another. 'It's a considerable distance.'

'That matters little. We'll hire a carriage from one of the hotels,' he returned briskly, striding towards a busy coaching inn on the far side of the street. 'Do you know the route to Keepers Ford, Keziah?'

'Yes, but I can't possibly go there now,' she answered earnestly. 'I'm collecting Edith from the rectory shortly, and then I need to make supper. Besides, I'd have to warn Pa and Gran if I'm to be out until late so they won't worry. I'm sorry, Benedict — I know you're trying to help.'

'There's no cause for apology, Keziah. It is I who am thoughtless,' he responded mildly. 'You have responsibilities, and a family depending upon you. Supposing I walk you home to the apothecary now, and call later with the carriage? This evening we'll drive to Keepers Ford, visit Mr Bell — and be a step nearer to locating the book.'

She nodded gratefully, and an hour was arranged for their meeting. When the apothecary came into sight, Benedict paused, his gloved hand resting lightly upon Keziah's sleeve.

'You have my word I will do everything possible to recover your grandmother's book, Keziah,' he began, adding with the ghost of a smile, 'I *also* promise we'll share that pot of the Wild Swan's most excellent tea and a dish of Yorkshire scones on another afternoon very soon indeed!'

* * ★

'What's going on, Keziah?'

Samuel confronted her in the seclusion of the hallway when she was taking off her cloak. 'I saw you outside the shop with the American — What are the pair of you plotting?'

She tossed her head and turned away, replying airily, 'Guilty conscience pricking you?'

'What's this about?' He grasped her arm with one hand, and with the other brandished the sheets of paper upon which Keziah had written draft versions of her letter to Joshua Bell. 'Why do you want to see Joshua Bell? It's about the book, isn't it?'

'What book might that be?' she challenged innocently, wresting free from the grip of his long, slender fingers. 'Whatever can you be talking about?'

'Don't play games, Keziah — '

'And don't you dare threaten me!' she retaliated, her eyes flashing angrily.

'I hold my tongue only to spare Gran and Pa's feelings! Benedict Clay, George and I know exactly what you did, Samuel, and Benedict is helping me set it to rights — *if* that be possible.

'You're despicable,' concluded Keziah, sweeping past him into the kitchen. 'Keep out of my sight, and consider yourself a very fortunate young man not to be exposed as the thief and liar you are!'

* * *

Perhaps Keziah's harsh words struck a chord within her younger brother's conscience, because she did not set eyes upon him again for the remainder of the afternoon. And immediately after the apothecary closed, Samuel quickly removed to his room.

When supper was ready and Keziah's call from the hallway brought no avail, she went upstairs to knock at her brother's door but on the landing met Elijah.

'Samuel went out a while back,' he remarked, starting downstairs for the evening meal. 'He's seeing Reverend Kennard and said he'd miss supper. Did he not tell you?'

'He did not.' Her lips compressed. Did Samuel genuinely have a meeting at St Harmon's with Reverend Kennard? Somehow Keziah doubted it.

'I'll set Samuel's meal aside,' she said, following Elijah down the stairs and adding caustically, 'I daresay he'll be hungry whenever he *does* come home!'

'There's nowt wrong with the lad's appetite, that's for sure,' Elijah went on, taking his place at table. 'I don't know where he packs it in, for there's nothing of him!'

'Samuel's wiry,' commented Meggan, setting the bread board into the middle of the table before taking her seat. 'He takes after his grandpa. My Frank was lean as a rake but my, he loved his food! Loved eating it and loved cooking it, too.'

'There never was a better chef in the whole of Harrogate, Meggan,' declared Elijah, helping Edith cut up her potatoes. 'Everybody said the same.'

'I like cooking,' remarked Edith, her small hands guided by her father's upon the knife and fork. 'Maybe I could be a cook like Grandpa . . .'

The family's amiable talk continued, however Keziah remained silent, anticipating Benedict's arrival, the imminent journey to Keepers Ford and their visit to Joshua Bell.

Benedict Clay arrived promptly, and with Meggan's warning to wrap up warm against the evening's cold wind ringing in her ears, Keziah took Benedict's hand and stepped up into the open-topped carriage, settling herself on the high, straight-backed seat and drawing the heavy woollen cloak close about her.

'This may not be the most comfortable transport,' he admitted, taking his place beside her and looping the worn reins through slender fingers. 'However it's light and robust, and the horses strong and swift, so we should make our journey in good time — All set?'

She looked across at him, the light from the flickering carriage lamps touching his lean face, and nodded. Drawing away from the apothecary and through the town, Clay deftly manoeuvred the steeply cobbled rise snaking around the castle's east walls and struck out into the rough, rutted drover's track towards Keepers Ford.

Presently, they approached the ford. Bringing the carriage to a halt and taking up one of the lamps, Benedict went ahead on foot, pausing at the crossing to gain a bearing on the depth of the murky, fast-flowing water. As she sat waiting, Keziah's thoughts inexplicably wandered to the moment their eyes had meet when he lifted her into the carriage, and the unexpected emotion that had surged within her during those brief moments she had been in his arms.

'The ford's swollen from so much

rainfall, but there's no cause for concern,' Benedict's soft voice broke into Keziah's reverie as he swung up onto the seat beside her, misreading her wistful expression. 'Try not to worry. All being well, this transaction will soon be resolved.'

The carriage traversed the swirling ford without difficulty and they drove on along a narrow winding lane bounded by hedgerow and overhung with gaunt, twisted trees.

'That must be Bell's cottage,' remarked Benedict, his shoulder brushing against Keziah's own as he pointed into the near distance. 'Over yonder, see?'

There was scant moon, and through the darkness Keziah could barely discern a distant smudge of whiteness beyond the gnarled black boughs of skeletal hawthorns. They drove onwards until they reached a broad break in the trees and a substantial white cottage slipped into sight. It stood in complete darkness. Not a single light burned at any of its small square panes. Benedict drew the carriage to a standstill.

'There are no signs of life.' He frowned. 'It doesn't look as if anyone's home.'

Guided only by the dull beams cast from the carriage lamps, Benedict took the horses up between the hawthorns and followed a curving, grit path around the cottage's frontage to a latticed porch heavy with evergreen.

All was still.

Of a sudden, Keziah was aware how very cold the night had become and she shuddered, huddling deeper into the folds of her woollen cloak. Somewhere close by, but beyond sight in the dark night, a horse whinnied and stamped and was answered by snorts and a shake of mane from the carriage horses, standing patient but restless while Benedict tied off the reins and jumped to the ground.

'Perhaps Mr Bell is at the rear of the cottage?' ventured Keziah optimistically, her hands upon his shoulders as he lifted her down.

'Perhaps,' remarked Benedict. Turning from her, he strode into the porch and reached for the bell-pull alongside the front door, drawing back sharply. 'Keziah — This door is open!'

At a slight touch from his hand, the low door swung wide and revealed a yawning well of absolute silence and total darkness. Benedict cautiously put a foot across the threshold, outstretching a protective hand toward Keziah to keep her at arm's length.

'Mr Bell!' He raised his voice a little, leaning into the shroud of blackness. 'Mr Joshua Bell? It's Miss Keziah Sephton and Benedict Clay! May we speak with you, sir?'

A prickle of unease crawled up Keziah's spine. She glanced over her shoulder to the paddock, where a grey horse had now entered the pool of dim light cast by the carriage lamps and was standing at the fence, ears back and eyes wide, scraping at the rough grass with its fore hoof and neighing. The grey's agitation elicited a responding call from one of the carriage horses while the second blew and shook her head, shifting her hoofs restlessly. It was obvious the animals were disturbed and Keziah shivered again, struck by foreboding.

'Something's wrong, Benedict!' she breathed urgently, hovering on the doorstone. 'Perhaps Mr Bell has been taken poorly. The stationer's clerk said he was an elderly gentleman — '

'Would you fetch a lamp from the carriage, Keziah?' interrupted Benedict, his voice low. 'There's no sense our blundering in when we can't see a hand before our faces!'

With the lantern held high, he started over the cottage's narrow threshold, muttering an oath as the stone flagging suddenly dropped away and he stumbled. 'Watch your footing there, Keziah!' he warned, quickly reaching back to catch hold of her arm. 'There's a steep step down onto the floor.'

Cautiously negotiating the flagstone,

she edged down to his side in the low-ceilinged hallway. A thick muffler hung from the stand; an umbrella and sturdy ash walking staff were propped alongside. A single glove lay upon a small square inlaid table, together with a folded newspaper and two unopened letters. Through an open door to their left was a small kitchen, spotlessly clean and tidy as a new pin. Without realising it, Keziah reached for Benedict's free hand, holding tightly onto his fingers as they crossed the hall towards a room facing them.

Its door was slightly ajar and Benedict gently nudged it open with the toe of his boot. With the first beam of lantern light falling into the large room, they could make out the bulk of heavy furniture, and walls lined by shelves neatly stacked with scores of books and journals.

'His study!' whispered Keziah, unaware she was whispering. 'The clerk said Mr Bell had been a master at the grammar school — '

She broke off with a shocked gasp as the lantern's beam swept the remainder of the room, touching upon a great oak desk set back beyond the fireplace.

Manuscripts, documents, pens, books, ink wells, correspondence and blotters had all been wantonly swept from the desk's surface and strewn to the stone flagged floor. A heavy crystal lamp lay overturned, spilling a shimmering puddle of oil across the mellow, well-polished oak. The lamp's tall, delicately-fluted chimney had been sent crashing against the hearth, splintering into a hundred glittering shards and scattering across a dark-stained glove that lay crumpled there.

The desk's drawers were wrenched from their runners and tipped out across the flags. Cupboards stood with doors flung wide, the shelves bare and their contents scattered to the ground.

'What the — ' began Benedict in disbelief, taking in the chaos. 'It's ransacked! Mr Bell's been burgled — '

'Yet the thief left *this!*' exclaimed Keziah, treading warily between the desk and fireplace to point at a fine old gold pocket watch hanging upon a hook at the side of the chimney breast. 'This watch is in plain sight so why — '

Her foot struck something solid and Keziah cried out, clutching the edge of the desk to steady herself. Benedict spun around to her, and in that instant a swinging splash of light illuminated the smooth grey flagstones behind the oak desk.

A crumpled body lay sprawled there.

A trickle of blood had dried and matted amongst the silver hair at the man's temple. Benedict swore softly, the lantern in his raised hand spilling flickering yellow light down upon the waxy features and staring eyes of Joshua Bell.

11

'The poor old gentleman,' muttered Keziah brokenly, twisting around in the high-backed seat and staring back to the neat white cottage while the carriage started away between the hedgerows. 'It's awful, to think of him lying there like that! We shouldn't leave him alone, Benedict.'

'We have no means of carrying his body,' reasoned Benedict, adding reflectively, 'We mustn't waste any time informing the law of his death, though. Is there a sheriff in Barrowby, Keziah? Or a town constable, perhaps?'

'Robert Towler.' She nodded distractedly, her eyes fixed upon the white cottage. 'Let me go back, Benedict! I don't mind staying with Mr Bell until the constable arrives. *Somebody* should be with him.'

'I agree it doesn't feel right leaving

him this way, but on the other hand, I'm not about to leave you alone either — not back there at the cottage or driving the carriage into town — not when there's a murderer on the loose!'

Keziah turned sharply to face him. It was the first time they'd actually spoken of *murder*. And yet, how else had the elderly schoolmaster met such a brutal death?

'A burglar must've forced his way into the cottage and attacked Mr Bell before making off with valuables,' she surmised slowly, then frowned, willing her mind to think logically. 'But if that were so, why didn't the thief steal the gold watch? It was in plain sight, hanging there by the chimney-piece. It surely would've been the first thing the thief would have seen after he'd — after he'd killed Mr Bell — wouldn't it?'

'Maybe . . . but suppose — just *suppose* — it happened the other way around, Keziah?' suggested Benedict, his eyes narrowing as he methodically recollected their every movement, and everything they had witnessed, at Joshua Bell's cottage. 'What if the old gentleman wasn't home when the thief broke in? None of the other rooms were ransacked, so perhaps the thief was only getting started searching for valuables when Mr Bell came back and disturbed him?'

'Yes, that has to be it,' she considered slowly, remembering something she'd hardly noticed at the time. 'Mr Bell was elderly. He'd doubtless take a walking stick with him whenever he went out. His walking stick was in the umbrella stand in the hall, yet Mr Bell was *still* wearing his outdoor clothes when we found him! One of his gloves was — was — ' Keziah's voice failed as the vivid image swam forcefully into her mind.

Swallowing hard, she pressed on with her reasoning. 'He must have returned home and gone indoors, Benedict. Put away his stick in the stand, took off his scarf and one of his gloves — Then perhaps he heard a noise, because he went straight into the study without taking off his coat!'

'And confronted an intruder searching his desk . . . Yes, that has to be it, Keziah!' exclaimed Benedict, adding uneasily, 'Which in a way, makes it the more curious a solid gold pocket watch be left behind. Once Mr Bell was silenced, the thief had all the time in the world to thoroughly search the whole house and bag everything with any value! *Why* didn't he do that?'

They drove on towards Barrowby without further speculation, each rapt within their thoughts. Keziah was increasingly distressed by the direction her own deliberations were taking. She didn't really believe it was possible, and was ashamed to be even harbouring such wicked notions. Nonetheless, the awful question would *not* be suppressed!

What if *Samuel* had ridden out to Keepers Ford this night?

What if . . . No. *No*, it could not be so!

Sammy might be irresponsible and reckless, but he never would harm . . . What if he were intoxicated and not himself, though?

Remembrance of that early morning in the kitchen at the apothecary sliced into her consciousness. Hadn't Keziah then felt threatened by her own brother's rage? Had she not feared while in the grip of such violent wrath he might strike her?

What if Samuel *had* called upon Mr Bell? Perhaps with an innocent intention of begging for the book's return? Instead, he'd found the cottage deserted and impulsively decided to find the Book of Hours and take it? Then, when Joshua Bell came home and confronted him, Samuel had panicked and —

'Here we are, Keziah.' Benedict's low voice broke into her anguish and she started, realising they were outside the apothecary and she was home. The shop was shut, but lamps were still burning within and she could see her father moving about behind the counter.

Elijah Sephton spotted them outside and smiling, came around to unlock the door for them. It only needed one look at his daughter's pale face and huge eyes, and a glance to Benedict Clay's grave countenance for him to realise something was badly amiss.

'We found an elderly gentleman deceased, sir. Out at Keepers Ford,' murmured Benedict quietly, pausing as Keziah moved towards the arch into the house before adding meaningfully, 'I must report his death to the constable, Mr Sephton. But Keziah needs — '

'Aye. Aye, lad, I understand. I'll go over to Constable Towler with you,' put in Elijah, ushering the younger man ahead of him from the shop. 'While I fetch summat for Kezzie, you away through to the kitchen. Meggan's already retired to her bed, but Samuel and young Betsy are in there . . . '

When the door opened and Keziah appeared on the threshold, Betsy

Sharples spun around from the kitchen table where she and Samuel were seated, heads together, deep in close conversation.

'Miss Keziah — Whatever's up? You look terrible!' Springing to her feet, Betsy darted to Keziah's side, drawing her towards the table. 'Sit yourself down — Tea's fresh-made. I'll fetch another cup.'

'Thanks, Betsy.' She gazed up at the girl gratefully, sinking down onto the straight-backed chair. Keziah's knees were suddenly jelly, and she couldn't quite manage to stop her voice and hands trembling. 'I do feel a bit all-in.'

Samuel was looking on, saying nothing. His apprehensive glance moved keenly from his sister's ashen face to Benedict Clay, standing protectively alongside her chair, and then to Elijah, emerging through the doorway with a soothing draught from the dispensary.

'Here, lass.' He offered the measure of pale liquid to Betsy as she poured Keziah's tea. 'Put five drops of that in;

it'll help her with the shock.'

Betsy did as she was bidden, pressing the tea-cup into Keziah's cold hands before looking up to the dark stranger who seemed to fill the homely kitchen with his presence. 'Can I get you some tea, sir?' she queried. 'There's plenty in the pot.'

'Thank you, no, ma'am. I have to leave directly,' Benedict responded, his hand resting lightly upon Keziah's shoulder. Looking down into her wide grey eyes, he murmured, 'Try to get some rest, Keziah. I'll come by tomorrow.'

'You'll — you'll attend to Mr Bell?' Reaching around, she clasped his hand as Benedict made to move away, desperately meeting his eyes, and biting back the almost overwhelming need to confide in him her fear Samuel was somehow involved in the elderly man's death. 'You *will* tell me what — whatever happens?'

'Of course. I'll come tomorrow,' he repeated softly, turning to quit the warm, comfortable kitchen and nodding politely to Betsy and Samuel. 'Ma'am. Samuel. Goodnight.'

Once he and Elijah Sephton were alone in the seclusion of the hallway, Benedict tersely explained what had occurred that evening, choosing not to elaborate upon the purpose of his and Keziah's visit to Keepers Ford.

'Dear Lord,' breathed Elijah, shaking his head in disbelief. 'Joshua Bell *murdered*!'

'My sincere apologies for not breaking the news more sensitively, sir!' responded Benedict immediately. 'I should have been mindful in a town this size, you'd likely be acquainted with the gentleman. Were you and Mr Bell close friends?'

'Nay . . . not what you'd call friends. But we'd known each other up'ards of twenty years, and got along well enough. Bell was a quiet sort. Kept himself to himself, 'specially after his wife passed away,' said Elijah. 'He didn't come into town very often, but

I'd sometimes see him at the reading room in Ormsley. He was a schoolmaster, th'knows. A keen reformer, too. We'd often-times meet at talks and debates at the institute over there.

'We fell into conversation about education once, and I was telling him about Sammy trying for a scholarship at York,' reflected Elijah, wrapping a muffler about his neck and reaching for his hat. 'Mr Bell offered to lend me books to help Sammy with his studies. Not for a fee, you understand — He never would take a penny-piece for his trouble. Whenever I offered, he'd just say helping a boy learn and make summat of himself was its own reward.'

'Your son also knew Mr Bell, then?'

Elijah shook his head. 'They met just the one time, when Sammy had won his scholarship and was off to York. He was only a little lad, but I took him with me to the reading room so he could thank Mr Bell for lending the books.

'For without his help, my son wouldn't

have got the first-rate education he's had, Mr Clay,' finished the apothecary quietly, crossing the deserted town square. 'Joshua Bell was a good man with a good heart. For him to be cut down like this . . . It's horrible. *Horrible!*'

'You mentioned Mr Bell was a widower,' began Benedict, allowing a few moments for the older man to compose himself. 'Had he any family, sir?'

'A daughter. Grandchildren too, I believe. Not in Barrowby, though. He had a brother as well. A clergyman,' recalled Elijah as they walked, hunched against the bitterly cold, driving rain. 'Augustus Bell. He came to the reading room once. If I recall rightly, he has a pit parish somewhere over Barnsley way.'

'Given that Keziah and I found Mr Bell,' sighed Benedict, 'I reckon I owe it to his kinfolk to take them news of his death — if you believe that would be appropriate, sir?'

'Aye, I do!' he responded, looking up

at the American with a new respect. 'It's decent of you to take on the responsibility, for it's a grim enough task for any man,' Elijah commented, as they approached the massive oak gates of the ruined castle's guardhouse. 'I can hardly believe it — Mr Bell bludgeoned to death in his own home! And you reckon it was done by a thief he caught in the act?'

'I have a hunch this whole tragedy is a lot more complicated than that,' opined Benedict Clay quietly, watching Elijah raise his hand and knock at the gate to summon the constable. 'We have no way of knowing what may have been stolen from Joshua Bell's cottage. His study was ransacked, but for what reason? Valuable goods in plain view were not stolen.

'If the intruder was searching for something in particular, Mr Sephton,' concluded Benedict, as Constable Towler drew open the mighty gate, 'he was prepared to murder an innocent man in cold blood to get it!'

After Keziah slowly climbed the stairs to her room, leaving Samuel and Betsy Sharples sitting quietly together in the warmly lit kitchen, she hadn't imagined sleep possible.

However she *had* slept, almost as soon as her head touched the pillow. She'd fallen into dreamless slumber, wakening with a dizzying jolt to find daylight filtering into her room and Meggan setting a breakfast tray onto the cabinet beside her bed.

'Gran — What hour is it?' Keziah exclaimed in alarm, immediately sitting bolt upright. She should have risen before dawn! 'I'm late! I must get Edith to school — '

'Nay, nay, lass — There's no call for fretting,' Meggan reassured, resting a hand to her granddaughter's shoulder and gently easing her back against the bolster. 'Samuel took Edie up to the rectory three hours since. Now bide and eat your breakfast.' Placing the tray across Keziah's knees, Meggan perched on the edge of the high bed. 'I thought we might talk a while.'

'You know about Mr Bell?'

'Your pa told me this morning. It's a terrible thing, Kezzie.' She shook her head, nudging the dish of porridge closer to Keziah and urging her to eat. 'I thank the good Lord you and young Benedict weren't harmed! It doesn't bear thinking on, if whoever killed that poor gentleman had been in the cottage when you got there.'

Meggan rose, disappearing from the room onto the landing, and returning a moment later bearing a bowl of fresh flowers.

'Benedict called first thing this morning asking after you and left these — Goodness knows how he came by such fine blooms this early in the year, but here they are!' Meggan smiled, setting the bowl onto the cabinet beside Keziah. 'He said he'd visit this afternoon, if that were convenient. Benedict seems such a genuine, kindly lad, and he has real, old-fashioned good manners about him, too.'

'I can't stay in bed, Gran!' protested Keziah, setting aside the tray. 'I should've been up hours ago. Why ever didn't you wake me? There're chores — '

'They're either being done, or they can wait a while longer!' countered Meggan firmly. 'Finding someone who's passed away is a shock nobody ever forgets, but what you and Benedict saw last night will take some getting over, Kezzie! Mark my words, sooner or later it will hit you like a ton of bricks. You need to keep your strength up or you'll be neither use nor ornament to yourself or anybody else. Eat your breakfast, there's a good lass.'

Keziah knew when she was beaten, and began the porridge.

'You say Samuel took Edith to school?' she queried as she ate, her mind flashing back to the strange expression upon her young brother's face when she'd told him and Betsy about Joshua Bell's murder. 'That isn't like Samuel! He usually has plans of his own — plans that do not involve this family.'

'You're too hard on the lad, Kezzie,' reproved Meggan, finishing her tea. 'I've told you so oft-times before.

'Sammy has his faults — as we all do — but his heart's in the right place. He mayn't have really known poor Mr Bell, but he knew of him, and about the help that gentleman gave him years ago. What's happened has hit Samuel hard. He feels things deep. Your Pa said when Benedict and him got back from seeing the constable, Sammy was sitting up waiting for them, wanting to hear if there were any news on who'd done it.'

'Was there?' Keziah heard her own voice enquiring, watching from lowered eyes as her grandmother slowly shook her head. 'Where is Samuel now?'

'Since he took Edith to school, he's not budged from behind that counter,' replied Meggan, with a little satisfied bob of her chin. 'And Sammy said you're to rest and not go down into the shop, for he'll be there all day and will fetch Edith home from the rectory, too.'

'That's quite a new leaf he's turned over,' remarked Keziah tartly, aware of Meggan's disapproving glance. 'But I'm not ill and I've slept quite long enough. Besides, I'd much rather be busy than moping about and — ' Unexpectedly, her voice faltered. ' — and thinking.'

'Aye, that's my way too.' Meggan nodded with a small sigh, fondly patting her granddaughter's mop of chestnut hair. 'Keeping busy is the best way. I'll leave you to get yourself up and dressed.'

★ ★ ★

Presently, Keziah went downstairs to the kitchen and she and Meggan got on with the chores. When Elijah went off with a fresh batch of medicines upon his routine daily call to the almshouse at Quarry End, Keziah slipped unnoticed into the shop and took her place beside Samuel.

He'd solicitously asked how she was feeling, and as the hours went by, Keziah became increasingly aware of Samuel's keen eyes upon her. She found it irritating. It was all she could do to hold her tongue and not berate him.

The apothecary was even busier than usual. Although Keepers Ford lay a distance outside the town and Joshua Bell had not been known to many folk, news of his murder had whipped around Barrowby in a frenzy of shock and speculation. Word of Keziah and the American stranger's involvement had also spread like flame through the town. Gossip and rumour were rife, and upon the lips of virtually every man and woman who crossed the apothecary threshold.

Some folk didn't even make pretence of requiring remedies and were plainly intent only upon quizzing Keziah. She knew she could have coped with the onslaught, had she been allowed to do so. As it was, Samuel hovered constantly, listening and watching, interrupting and politely thwarting the barrage of questions bombarding his sister.

' . . . My father and Mr Bell were known to one another for a number of years, and I owed the gentleman a great debt of gratitude for his guidance and knowledge. As you're doubtless aware, my sister and our cousin from overseas discovered Mr Bell's death,' repeated Samuel over and again throughout that day, adding with an intonation that brooked no opposition, 'I'm sure you appreciate Keziah cannot discuss events from last evening, however I will be pleased to attend to your medicinal requirements.

'How may Sephton's Apothecary help you today . . . ?'

* * *

The day wore on, with brother and sister having no opportunity for conversation.

Keziah felt like she wasn't really in

the shop at all. Her thoughts and senses were out at Joshua Bell's isolated cottage. Walking into the study. Seeing him there. Over and over again, she saw him. Couldn't stop thinking about seeing him. Over and over and over . . .

Her head had been aching for hours and as Keziah checked orders in the stock book, the neat black figures blurred out of focus before her eyes. Closing the thick ledger, she briefly rested both palms upon the well-worn cover.

'I'm going to make some tea, Sammy. Would you like a cup bringing — ' she began, breaking off as the brass bell jangled noisily yet again. Upon this occasion, however, it was George Cunliffe who strode inside, his ruddy face creased with concern. Although less than twenty-four hours had passed since Keziah last saw him, George looked thoroughly exhausted, as though he hadn't had any sleep for days.

'Are you alright, Kez?' he demanded at once. 'I met your pa on his way to

Quarry End and he told me what happened — '

'I'm — ' faltered Keziah. Before she could reply further, Samuel interrupted quietly.

'Why don't you and George go through and make that tea?' he suggested, lightly touching his sister's forearm. 'I can manage perfectly well out here.'

'Thank you, Sammy,' murmured Keziah uncertainly, looking up into her younger brother's handsome face and trying to read the inscrutable expression in his eyes. 'You'll call me, if I'm needed?'

' . . . Kez, I knew nothing about the old man until just now! I left town before daylight this morning on a job for Erskine's and have only just got back,' George began the instant they were alone in the kitchen with the hallway door snugly closed behind them. 'Everybody's talking about it — and saying *you* found the body!

'Then I spotted your pa and he told

me it was true! That you and that American *had* been to the old man's cottage. I came straight round. Are you alright?' he repeated earnestly. 'Did you catch sight of the culprit?'

Keziah shook her head, her hands busy setting out cups. 'It was pitch-dark when we got there. Everywhere was in darkness. There was nobody. Except — except Mr Bell.'

Heaving a sigh of relief, George went to her side and put his arm about her shoulders. 'Thank God you're safe! You could've walked in on whoever did it!' He sucked in a hoarse breath. 'Did the old man say anything to you before he . . . passed on?'

'We were too late, George. He was already dead,' she mumbled, not meeting George's eyes as she half-turned, bending to place the kettle onto the hob and pushing it over the glowing coals. 'Mr Bell was lying on the floor . . . There was blood — his blood all over . . . '

'Here now, here now, you sit down

before you fall down,' he urged, shepherding her to a chair. 'You're white as a sheet, and not surprising after what you've been through. I'll see to mashing the tea.'

They sat together quietly, sipping the hot, strong, sweet tea.

'How was your trip to Hawbeck?' asked Keziah at length. 'Were any of the roads to Hawbeck flooded? Keepers Ford was very deep. The horses almost waded across.'

'I managed alright, bit slower than I would've liked. I got the job done, though, so Erskine's got nowt to complain about — not as that that'll stop his moaning.' George shrugged, his face stony as he went on. 'What were you doing out there at Keepers Ford, Kez? You and me had arranged to go together this morning. What were you doing in the middle of nowhere late at night with a total stranger? The whole town's gossiping about the pair of you!'

'Then shame on it!' snapped Keziah, her grey eyes sparking behind a mist of furious tears. 'A man *died* last night, George!

'And I'm not about to argue with you again about being in Benedict Clay's company,' she went on, meeting George's accusing gaze defiantly. 'Surely we put *that* subject to rest after the appalling scene you made outside Pearce's tea-room!'

'You and me were fixing to see the old man together this morning,' persisted George bitterly. 'How come you went on your own with the American last night? That's all I'm asking, Kez! Surely I can ask you a question, can't I?'

'The why of it is simple enough,' responded Keziah wearily, recounting the previous day's events. ' . . . Somehow, yesterday seems a very long time ago now! Your driving off to Hawbeck, my sending the note to Joshua Bell and being on pins for hours afterwards awaiting his reply . . .

'When it finally came with the boy from the Rose and Crown, Mr Bell's letter was extremely kind and courteous — I have it here.' She took the crumpled sheet from her pocket. 'However, he no longer had the book in his possession. Read it for yourself.'

George scanned the fluent lines in disbelief, unable to take his eyes from the dead man's letter.

'So all that fuss . . . and Bell didn't even *have* the book!' he exclaimed, then suddenly looked at Keziah keenly. 'What'd he done with it?'

'How would I know?' she retorted sharply, taking the letter and folding it into her pocket once more.

'If you knew the old man didn't have the book,' challenged George suspiciously, 'What reason had you for going out to Keepers Ford with Clay?'

'Because I wanted to ask Mr Bell where the book was!' she cried in sheer exasperation. 'Lest there was any possibility of getting it back. And since the book had changed hands so swiftly, Benedict believed there was no time to be lost in learning its whereabouts so

242

we could track it down.'

'*Benedict!*' George almost spat the name in disgust. 'You couldn't wait till morning to go with me like we planned, could you? Oh, no, *you* had to set off on a wild goose chase alone with *him!*'

'This is ridiculous!' she countered impatiently. 'You're deliberately twisting everything to suit what you choose to believe! Do you not understand none of that even *matters?*

'A man was brutally murdered last night, George — ' Keziah paused, rigid-backed and glaring across the quiet kitchen at him. 'Isn't his death rather more important than your petty jealousies?'

★ ★ ★

Later that afternoon, Elijah and Samuel were working together in the apothecary and turned around in surprise at sight of Keziah emerging through the arch clad in bonnet, warmest cloak and mittens.

'I'll collect Edith from the rectory,' she began, going on as her father and brother simultaneously drew breath to object. 'It's too early yet, I know, but I'd like to sit a while in St Harmon's before Edie finishes her lessons.'

'Aye, lass, of course,' nodded Elijah, his gentle smile filled with understanding. 'You take your time.'

Sombre thoughts accompanied Keziah during the lengthy walk through the town and up towards Castlehill, where St Harmon's stood on high ground overseeing the parish of Barrowby.

After praying, Keziah rose and stood alone in the quietude, the stillness of the old church at odds with the turmoil engulfing her senses. At length, she moved noiselessly through the nave and past the great carved font to draw open the heavy west door, hesitating there a moment before stepping out into the keen wind cutting down from the distant hills.

She'd taken but a step or two along the winding churchyard path before she saw Benedict Clay emerging from the shadows of the lych-gate. He'd clearly been waiting there, and now raised a hand in greeting before starting towards her.

'I've come from the apothecary,' he explained after enquiring upon Keziah's wellbeing. 'Samuel said I'd find you here. I hope I'm not intruding?'

'Of course not!' she responded sincerely, immeasurably consoled by his unexpected appearance. 'Is — is there any news?'

'Not yet,' answered Benedict, going on with uncharacteristic awkwardness. 'After what's happened, I couldn't just leave . . . That is, I didn't *want* to leave until — ' He broke off, concluding simply, 'I've sent word ahead to Liverpool for my ship to sail without me, Keziah. I'll be staying in England until this is over.'

'I'm so glad!' she mumbled, almost overcome. 'And I'm so very glad to see

you, Benedict! I can't stop thinking . . . '

She felt his hand gently taking her
arm, and try as she did, suddenly
Keziah could no longer stem the tears
that had been threatening since their
discovery of Joshua Bell's body.

'Shall we step inside?' Benedict
murmured, offering his handkerchief
and guiding Keziah back towards the
west door and into the church.

They sat there together, enveloped in
the silence and solace of centuries. It
was Keziah who finally spoke.

'Has the culprit been caught, Benedict?'

He shook his head. 'Your father
— and everyone else I've spoken to who
knew Mr Bell — says the exact same
thing. He was a scholarly, greatly
respected old gentleman who lived
alone and quietly with his books. He
certainly didn't have any enemies or
anybody who would wish to harm him.
This morning, I returned to his cottage
with Constable Towler — '

'You've been back?' she cried in consternation. 'Why — '

'I wanted to *do* something,' he interrupted softly. 'Last night, your father and I talked a good deal, Keziah. He told me Mr Bell has a daughter and an elder brother, a clergyman. While I was at Keepers Ford today, I got their addresses from letters they'd written — '

'There were letters on the hall stand!' gasped Keziah, remembering. 'Mr Bell must've been into town to collect his mail — Oh! Were those letters from his family?'

'One was from his daughter,' answered Benedict simply. 'Since there isn't anyone else to do so, I'm taking it upon myself to call upon Mr Bell's daughter and brother to break the news. Neither lives nearby, so I propose travelling with the next east-bound stage from the Rose and Crown.

'It departs in a few hours,' he went on quietly. 'I wanted to see you before I leave.'

She nodded wordlessly, tears brimming again but remaining unshed as the two rose from the pew and started from the church.

'Pa mentioned he thought Mr Bell's daughter lived up at Goathland,' Keziah began, when they paused at the rectory path before parting. 'It's a very long journey across the moors, Benedict, and I hear the road is lonely and dangerous. Please come back safe!'

'I will,' was all he said at first, holding her gaze a long moment before continuing softly, 'I've travelled thousands of miles, Keziah, and now, suddenly, all I've been seeking is — '

Benedict was interrupted by brisk rapping upon the oblong pane of one of the rectory's side windows. As one, he and Keziah looked around to see Reverend Kennard purposefully attracting their attention and indicating they go around to the front door. When they did so, he was waiting there and bid them enter.

Cyril Kennard was a tall, lantern-jawed man in middle years with a melancholic countenance and a disposition that routed out wickedness everywhere. He had neither time nor patience for pleasantries, immediately enlisting Keziah and her grandmother's needlecraft skills to repair and restore the embroidery on several tapestry kneelers belonging to the Baldwin family pew.

Satisfied the sewing-work would soon be underway, Mr Kennard produced a bundle of faded music and told Keziah be sure and deliver it to Samuel without delay. 'I intended lending this to him when he was here practising last evening,' explained the vicar. 'Unfortunately, I was detained elsewhere on important parish business so wasn't able to see your brother.

'There'll now be music for Joshua Bell's funeral to be arranged too, of course,' he ruminated with a slow shake of the head. 'Bell and I were both keen horticulturists, you know. I shall miss our discussions.'

Reverend Kennard's attention suddenly turned upon Benedict, his gimlet-gaze boring into the younger man. 'What news have you of the murder, Mr Clay?'

'Very little, I regret to say,' replied Benedict. 'It appears Mr Bell returned home and disturbed an intruder.'

'And the thief killed him before making his escape,' surmised Kennard grimly. 'Bell wasn't a wealthy man, but he did have a number of valuable possessions. How much was stolen, Mr Clay? The daily woman who went in to cook and clean would surely be able to provide an accurate list of goods missing?'

'Mrs Wickes has indeed been very helpful,' agreed Benedict soberly. 'I was with Constable Towler when he spoke to her. Upset as the poor woman was, she went around Mr Bell's cottage and was certain nothing was missing. Only the study had been disturbed.'

'I believe the gold watch Bell

inherited from his father and kept hanging at the chimney-piece was left untouched? Curious, curious. It's a queer sort of thief that kills a man, yet leaves with empty pockets!' opined Reverend Kennard, as muffled voices and footsteps approached from within the rectory. 'Ah, the pupils have finished their lessons for the day! I'll bid you both farewell — You will be sure to give Samuel that music without delay, won't you, Miss Sephton . . . ?'

The vicar vanished indoors, while Keziah and Benedict walked a little distance down the path to await Edith and the other children, who were already emerging in orderly fashion from the rectory doorway.

'Mr Bell hadn't any enemies and nothing was stolen from his cottage,' began Keziah hurriedly, wishing to speak before her young sister joined them. 'What is it you know that you're not telling me, Benedict?'

He shrugged. 'I don't know any more than you do, Keziah.'

'A queer sort of thief indeed, who kills and frantically searches, yet takes nothing,' she persisted rapidly. 'Unless the one item he seeks is no longer in the cottage to be found!'

Keziah's throat was dry. Afraid as she was to give credence to the question burning in her mind, she could not leave it unasked.

'Do you think the Book of Hours has anything to do with Mr Bell's murder?'

Benedict Clay met her fearful eyes steadily. 'I'm sorry to tell you, Keziah, but I do believe your grandmother's book is at the very heart of this tragedy.'

12

At Benedict's behest, Keziah did not see him off aboard the east-bound coach.

However, while she sat in the parlour helping Edith with her cross-stitching, Keziah heard the distant bellow of the post-horn and in her mind's eye, envisaged the grimy, mud-spattered coach rattling through the streets of Barrowby and away towards the desolate moors. It wouldn't reach Goathland until the morrow, and after visiting Mr Bell's daughter, Benedict intended travelling south-west down across to Barnsley, where Reverend Augustus Bell had a living within a busy mining community. Benedict had warned Keziah he didn't foresee returning to Barrowby before the week's end.

Presently, Keziah left Edith cross-stitching her sampler at the fireside and went into the kitchen to lend Meggan a hand preparing supper.

'You look right peaky, lass,' opined her grandmother bluntly. 'And there's no point saying you're alright, because you're not! Nobody would be. This'll take its toll, so make sure you look after yourself.' Meggan's expression softened and she smiled, elbowing Keziah in the ribs. 'You're the stalwart in this family, Kezzie. If you fall poorly, the rest of us will be in a right pickle!'

With the evening meal underway, Keziah popped her head around the parlour door. 'Edith, put away your sewing now and set the table! Pa and Samuel are both in, so a place for all of us.'

'And one extra!' called Meggan, stirring custard and watching a simmering pot at the same time. 'George called in while you were collecting Edie from the rectory,' she went on, when Keziah looked around in surprise. 'Your pa asked him for supper. There's nowt wrong between the pair of you, is there?'

Keziah shook her head, but while she and George hadn't exactly quarrelled that morning, they hadn't parted on the best of terms either. And she regretted that. 'I'm glad he's coming, Gran. We've things to talk about.'

'I'm sure.' She sighed. 'He's a good man, Kezzie. You'll not find one as works harder to better himself, either. I wish George *could* buy the yard! After the graft he's put into that business, it's only what he deserves. It'd be the making of the lad, too.'

The subject of Erskine's came up again almost as soon as they were gathered together for supper.

'. . . I'm sorry to eat and run,' began George apologetically, appreciatively surveying the meal about to be put on the table. 'Mr Erskine got a last minute job — a favour for one of his church cronies — and wants it doing tonight. It's a long drive, so after I've picked up the goods, I'll grab a few hours' shut-eye in the waggon before starting home.

'Long as I'm back in time to open up the yard,' he finished bitterly, helping himself to roasted potatoes. 'Erskine won't have owt to complain about — for a change!'

Meggan tutted sympathetically. 'Kezzie and me were only saying earlier on, how Stanley Erskine should be thankful he has someone honest and reliable as you working for him!'

'Ah, he's not so bad, I suppose, Mrs Worsley. He gave me a job when nobody else would,' remarked George with a resigned sigh. 'I owe him for that. Work's work, when all's said and done.'

'If Erskine *is* fixing to sell — and I've not heard anything definite one way or t'other,' put in Elijah mildly, 'it'd only be proper for him to offer you the yard at a fair price, George.'

'I've some brass saved, Mr Sephton, but it'd be a drop in the ocean. I once asked Erskine about buying into the business,' George answered resentfully, his attention fixed upon the meal before him. 'He laughed in my face.'

Their conversation uneasily moved on. As though by tacit agreement, the mystery surrounding the death of Joshua Bell was not spoken upon.

It wasn't until supper was over, and Keziah was showing George out through the apothecary, that events of the previous night were mentioned.

'Kez, I'm sorry for the way — for what I said — about you being out with the American,' began George awkwardly, turning his hat between his hands as he faced her in the dimly lit shop. 'I spoke out of turn, and I apologise humbly.'

'Oh, George!' she murmured hopelessly. 'There are thoughts . . . *awful thoughts* . . . I cannot put from my mind!'

He reached out, clasping her shoulders firmly. When George finally spoke, his voice was perfectly calm. 'You're wondering if Samuel had anything to do with what happened at Keepers Ford, aren't you?'

Keziah looked away. 'I can't believe him capable of such a deed.'

'No, but you're thinking Sam's not been himself of late,' George proffered gently. 'He's even threatened you a couple of times . . . Try as you will, you'll not shut out them thoughts, Kez.'

'I can't believe it — I can't and I *won't* — but,' she confided miserably, 'but what if Samuel *is* somehow responsible, George? He wouldn't deliberately have harmed the old gentleman, I *know* he wouldn't, but suppose it happened by accident?

'Perhaps Sammy was there at the cottage and he and Mr Bell were talking and Mr Bell collapsed or stumbled or something and cracked his head on the flags.'

'Samuel had found out Bell had the book . . . Maybe he *did* go there last night to get it back,' reasoned George slowly. 'Happen there was an argument, the old man fell or some such as you say, the lad panicked and ran off.' He paused. 'Have you said anything to him, Kez?'

'I haven't had a chance. Samuel's scarcely set foot from the shop all day,' she answered in despair. 'There's something else —

'Last evening, Samuel went out before supper.' Keziah hesitated. 'He told Pa he was going to St Harmon's to practice the Easter music — '

'Then you've been worrying over nowt, haven't you!' exclaimed George, smiling broadly. 'Not even your clever-clogs brother can be in two places at once!'

'That's just it,' countered Keziah despondently. 'Mr Kennard wasn't at *church* last night!'

'There's no proof Samuel was at the church either then?' sighed George, touching Keziah's arm consolingly. 'Aye . . . I must admit, it does look bad for him! Mind, even if Sam *had* looked in at the church last evening, a good fast horse could have taken him across country to Keepers Ford in next to no time —

'But no!' he declared stoutly. 'This is plain daft, Kez! It's your *brother* we're talking about! I just can't believe Sam killed that old man. The lad may have a hot head and a quick temper, but drunk or sober, he'd never do summat like that!

'There's only one thing'll set your mind at rest, though, Kez,' concluded George practically. 'Have it out with Sam! Hear what he has to say and clear the air between the pair of you.'

'I'll speak to him later.' She frowned, her eyes troubled. 'After Pa's gone into the parlour with his pipe and the newspaper and Gran has gone up to bed. Sammy and I will be alone then.'

'It'll sort itself out, Kez,' reassured George, squeezing her hand. 'Look, I don't like rushing off when you're in a state, but Erskine will have my hide if I don't get this furniture picked up — It's for Cyril Kennard, and you know how thick him and the vicar are!'

'I wish you *could* buy out Stanley

Erskine.' She gazed up at him ruefully. 'Gran and Pa were absolutely right — It's thanks to you the business is a prosperous concern. It's only fair you have the chance to take over!'

'Aye, well what's fair in life and what we end up with are two different things,' remarked George bitterly, turning to the door but glancing back at her with his familiar grin. 'What I need is a windfall, Kez, and the only windfall I'm likely to ever get is apples dropping off the trees come harvest-time!'

* * *

When Keziah went back into the house, she found Samuel sitting at their mother's upright little piano, softly playing an old folk song. He looked up immediately Keziah entered the room and got to his feet, as though he'd been awaiting her return. Before she could speak, he said, 'I want to tell you something, Kezzie. I've wanted to say it the whole day long, but there hasn't been a chance to — '

'I know.' She met Samuel's plaintive eyes, and Keziah knew having faith in her brother's innate goodness was not misplaced. With all her heart she believed him innocent of any crime. 'Why don't I make us some chocolate?'

The kitchen fire had been banked up for the night so the homely room was already becoming chill. Steam from the jug of chocolate rose in wisps as Keziah poured their drinks, then she and Samuel settled together across the scrubbed oak table.

'When you came in with Benedict last night,' he began, running his tongue over dry lips, 'I'd already owned up to Granny and Pa about taking — *stealing* — the book, and the takings from the cash-box.

'They were . . . quite wonderful. Both of them,' pressed on Samuel, shame-faced. 'They've forgiven me, Kezzie. I don't deserve it.'

'You've told them the *truth*, Sammy!'

she replied warmly. 'Now you can begin making amends!'

'How can I ever put right the wrongs I've committed?' he demanded scathingly. 'I can't *undo* taking the family's money from the cash-box nor stealing Gran's book from her, can I?

'When I discovered those drafts of the letter you'd written and found Mr Bell had bought the book, all I could think about was raising enough money to buy it back,' went on Samuel agitatedly. 'I went straight to Castle-hill — '

'You didn't go to St Harmon's?' interrupted Keziah quietly.

He shook his head. 'I *had* to get that money, Kezzie! I called on the Baldwin brothers and asked — *begged* — for a loan.

'They were playing chess and didn't even pause their game while I was explaining,' recalled Samuel harshly. 'When I'd finished, Percy remarked what a rotten sport I was, down on my

263

luck, and rang for the maid to show me out!

'I've been such a colossal fool — worse than a fool! — because I actually believed the Baldwins were my *friends!*'

'It's fortunate you've seen their colours sooner rather than later,' she said sensibly, adding mildly, 'There is another who truly *does* care for you, Sammy. Someone genuinely deserving of your trust and friendship — if you will but pay mind!'

'Betsy,' he acknowledged with a pensive smile. 'I've been taking Betsy for granted, Kezzie, yet she's stood by me and never once let me down!

'Last night, when I was at the Baldwins', the maid told Betsy I was there so she sneaked around from the servants' quarters and was waiting for me when I was shown out at the front door. We came home together,' Samuel continued quietly. 'Betsy's a very forthright person, Kezzie. She lost no time telling me a good many home truths and made me really *look* at the kind of man I'd become. I didn't like what I saw.'

'You've told her about taking Gran's book and the money?' queried Keziah in surprise.

'Betsy was the only one I *could* tell!' he confessed. 'We've been the best of friends since we were Edie's age, and Betsy *knew* something was terribly wrong. She asked me straight out, and I told her everything.'

'Betsy Sharples is a fine young woman,' responded Keziah sincerely, certain the girl had played a huge role helping Samuel find sufficient courage to own his misdeeds to Gran and Pa. 'And she has the highest regard for you!'

'I know, as do I for her.' Samuel smiled for the first time. 'Betsy's the only girl for me and always has been — I've been too much of a fool to realise — '

He broke off at quiet footsteps approaching from across the yard, then there came a gentle tap at the back door.

It was uncommonly late for visitors and Keziah rose apprehensively, her first thought being that for some reason Benedict had returned unexpectedly. However, when she lifted the latch and drew open the door, it was Cyril Kennard standing there on the threshold.

'Mr Kennard!' she exclaimed, taken aback.

'Forgive my calling at this hour, Miss Sephton,' he began, removing his hat and entering the candle-lit kitchen. 'I have spent the evening in prayer for Mr Bell, and in contemplation of his funeral service.

'I wish to speak with Samuel, if that be convenient?'

Samuel was on his feet, his pale features drawn as he extended a hand to accept the clergyman's greeting. 'Good evening, sir! Won't you be seated?'

'Can I get you some tea, Vicar?'

enquired Keziah, quickly clearing the chocolate cups and jug from the table. 'Or coffee, perhaps?'

He shook his head. 'Nothing for me, thank you.'

'I shall leave you to your discussion,' murmured Keziah, exchanging an encouraging glance with Samuel. 'Goodnight, Mr Kennard.'

She noiselessly quit the kitchen, closing the door quietly behind her and climbing the steep stairs, wondering what manner of church business had brought Reverend Kennard from the rectory at this hour of night.

Repairing to her room, Keziah lit the lamp and settled to her sewing. The house was quite silent. No murmur of solemn voices drifted up from the kitchen to reach her ears, and the long case clock at the foot of the stairs chimed two quarters before Keziah heard a door opening and closing, then the creak of the stairs as Samuel came up. His customary lithe, brisk step sounded heavy and ponderous.

Neatly folding her needlework, Keziah crossed her room and drew open the door as Samuel was reaching the landing.

'Is anything wrong?' she whispered, concerned at her young brother's grief-stricken expression. 'What is it, Sammy? What did Mr Kennard want with you at this time of night?'

'It seems the vicar and Mr Bell were close friends, Kezzie.' He drew in a halting breath before continuing. 'Apparently, they shared interests in gardening and music. Attended concerts together at Harrogate and York.

'Mr Kennard knew about Mr Bell's helping me with my studies when I was a boy and he's asked me to play at the funeral,' mumbled Samuel, his lowered eyes upon a neatly bound portfolio of music in his hands. 'These pieces are — were — some of Mr Bell's favourite . . .'

'Oh, Sammy!' she reached up, gently touching his cold cheek. 'It's so very sad, but such an honour too! And a special way for you to express your gratitude for the help Mr Bell gave you.'

Overcome with emotion, Samuel was unable to reply and Keziah's heart went out to her brother as he stood before her on the shadow-washed landing, looking so vulnerable, scared and so very, very young.

'What will you play?' she whispered softly.

'The Bach, I think,' he murmured at length. 'Yes, the Bach . . . '

And silent tears slid from Samuel's lowered eyes.

13

On the eve of Joshua Bell's funeral, Reverend Kennard paid another sombre visit to the apothecary and introduced Augustus Bell to the Sephton family, who were gathered in the parlour, together with Benedict Clay and Betsy Sharples.

'I wish to thank you again, Mr Clay,' began Reverend Bell, after they were seated and Keziah and Betsy had brought in tea. 'Your compassion toward my niece and her family and myself in delivering the sad news of Joshua's death is greatly appreciated. Anne — Mrs Lathom — has asked me to offer her kindest regards and gratitude to you.' The elderly clergyman now looked to Keziah. 'And of course to Miss Sephton, also.'

'These must be the very worst of days for her,' murmured Keziah gently.

'Are Mrs Lathom and her family arrived in Barrowby yet?'

Augustus Bell nodded, sipping his tea. 'They've put up at the Wild Swan. I endeavoured to persuade Anne to leave her children at home in Goathland, but she and Mr Lathom were most determined their family would not be parted at this time.'

'I can understand the poor lass feeling that way,' reflected Meggan, the sad conversation stirring memories of her own losses. 'It's times like these when folk need the strength of being together with loved ones. How old are the bairns?'

'Harold is seven and little Mattie almost five, Mrs Worsley. They had been looking forward to coming to see their grandfather when the weather for travelling improved,' he sighed, adding, 'Anne wished to visit Joshua's cottage today, but fortunately Mr Lathom and I were able to dissuade her. There'll be sufficient opportunity after the funeral.'

'I believe you're staying at the cottage

yourself, sir?' put in Elijah quietly. 'You will let us know if we can lend a hand with anything?'

'Much obliged, Mr Sephton. Much obliged,' responded Augustus, taking in the sympathetic family gathered about the snug parlour with its mellow-burning lamps and welcoming fireside. 'Although there was of course much not right at the cottage, when I arrived in Barrowby, there was no place else I thought to lodge but at Joshua's own home.

'I spoke to Constable Towler earlier,' concluded the clergyman sombrely. 'There is no sign of the perpetrator of the crime being found and brought to justice.'

★   ★   ★

' . . . I don't see why we had to come to the funeral,' George was grumbling as he and Keziah slowly followed Elijah, Benedict Clay, Samuel and Betsy Sharples along the curving path through the churchyard towards the great west door of St Harmon's. Meggan had chosen to remain at home with Edith, and Sephtons' Apothecary had closed as a mark of respect upon the day Joshua Bell was to be laid to his rest.

George fidgeted with his stiffly starched white collar, his gaze fixed on the open west door and the cavernous darkness into which the silent procession of mourners was gradually absorbed.

'It's not like you even knew the old man, Kez!'

'I'm here to pay my respects to Mr Bell,' she snapped softly, glaring at him sidelong. 'As is everybody present! Besides, it was Reverend Bell and Mrs Lathom's particular wish Benedict and my family and I be here.

'And bearing in mind it was Benedict and I who found — '

'Oh, I'm hardly likely to forget *that*, am I?' cut in George curtly, adjusting his borrowed tall black hat. 'I'm never done hearing about it!'

'Why are you being this way? Today, of all days?' demanded Keziah sharply. The bells of the old church were tolling, their sonorous peal carrying on the cold, clear morning air far across Barrowby town, out past the quarry pits and the almshouse, away to the distant, bare hills beyond the river.

'You've done nothing but complain about the funeral and having to ask Mr Erskine for a few hours off! You patently don't wish to attend, George, so why have you insisted upon doing so? I told you days ago, the Sephtons would be coming as a family — There was no need whatsoever for your accompanying me!'

'Like I was going to let you come on your own,' retorted George, taking off his hat as they entered the church and at the same moment jerking his head in Benedict Clay's direction. 'And give *him* the opportunity to step in offering his arm!'

Keziah was no longer listening to George's acrimonious words.

Her sorrow-filled gaze was resting upon Joshua Bell's bereaved little family. Keziah hadn't yet met Anne Lathom or her husband and children, but was deeply moved by thoughts of Mr Bell's only daughter making a long and desolate journey back to her childhood home to arrange for the burial of her beloved father.

Swallowing the lump in her throat, Keziah became aware of Samuel's moving away from Betsy's side in the nave and up towards the chancel steps, in preparation for his playing the requiem music. Elijah paused in the aisle, shepherding first Betsy and Benedict, and then Keziah and George, along one of the high-sided pews before taking his own place.

Cyril Kennard and Augustus Bell were standing together before the altar. In the moments before the service began, Keziah glanced to her right and found Benedict Clay's eyes, darker and deeper than ever in the dimly lit church, looking at her and watching her.

Watching over her!

The notion came unbidden to Keziah's thoughts, and unaccountably she felt comforted.

Samuel rose to his feet, drawing his bow and the first solemn notes of the Bach soared up to the high vaulted roof, reverberating around the oak beams and weathered stones of the thirteenth-century church. All thoughts were banished from Keziah's mind save those for the family grieving at Joshua Bell's simple coffin. She could not begin to imagine the pain Anne Lathom was silently enduring as she stood there with bowed head, saying her final good-bye . . .

When the service ended and the mourners were slowly departing the graveside, Benedict lingered, engaged in quiet conversation with Reverends Kennard and Bell, while Keziah and George, accompanied by Samuel, Betsy and Elijah, started towards the path. Mr and Mrs Lathom and their children were gathered near the west door and as the Sephtons approached, Anne Lathom stepped forward.

'Miss Sephton.' She spoke a little unsteadily, extending her hand. 'Thank you so much for coming, and for everything you and Mr Clay have done for our family since my father's death . . . I only wish we could have met upon a happier occasion.'

'Indeed so, Mrs Lathom,' responded Keziah, gently clasping the grieving woman's gloved hand. 'My condolences, and those of my family — ' She commenced introducing everyone, concluding with George.

'Are you from Keepers Ford, Mr Cunliffe?' enquired Anne Lathom politely. 'Did you know my father well?'

'I didn't, ma'am. Not at all, I'm afraid,' replied George, bowing his head as he briefly took Anne's hand. 'I never actually met Mr Bell, nor been out Keepers Ford way either, as a matter of fact. But like all the other folk here, I wanted to pay my respects, ma'am.'

At that juncture, Benedict in company with Cyril Kennard and Augustus Bell re-joined the Sephtons, while Anne and her husband proceeded down the winding path through the churchyard towards their carriage.

'Miss Sephton,' Augustus Bell began quietly, his gaze lingering a moment longer upon the progression of the funerary cortege before meeting Keziah's eyes. 'Miss Sephton, I need to speak with you upon a private matter. As you are aware, I'm staying in my brother's cottage at Keepers Ford and would be obliged if you will come to tea there tomorrow afternoon?

'Reverend Kennard and Mr Clay are privy to the matter for discussion, and will be in attendance.' The elderly clergyman paused. 'It is of considerable importance, Miss Sephton. Will you please join us?'

'Why — why, yes. Of course,' she responded, taken aback by the curious invitation and quickly darting an enquiring glance to Benedict. He was standing a little away from her, clearly in company and in confidence with the two clergymen.

Benedict Clay's impassive expression, however, revealed nothing.

★   ★   ★

'What I'd like to know,' George complained as he drove Keziah from Barrowby out towards Keepers Ford the following afternoon, 'is what sort of daftness this tea party's about? Bell's brother asking you out to his cottage! What can *he* have to talk to *you* about — and why didn't he invite me as well, Kez?

'Or your pa, or your brother, for that matter?' went on George suspiciously. 'It's a rum do, if you ask me! Clergyman or no, he's a total stranger and it's not right an old man like him asking a young lass to go to his house on her own!'

'Oh, for heaven's sake! Don't be ridiculous, George — You're making the invitation sound improper,' she responded impatiently. 'Benedict and Reverend Kennard are to be present!'

'So Augustus Bell says!' snorted George, snapping the reins so the horse quickened its pace. 'Just get it over and done as quick as you can, Kez, for I've better things to do than waste time supping tea with churchmen — even if you haven't!'

Keziah cast him a sharp glance, but bit back the scathing retort on the tip of her tongue.

George had been peculiarly out of sorts these past days. Moreover, Keziah felt recently there had been an increasing distance extending between them and that rather than being with her because he desired her companionship, George had kept Keziah's company merely from habit, as something which was expected of him.

As a *duty*, almost.

Of course, Keziah reasoned, there was indeed much to vex George's mind at present. The imminent prospect of

Erskine's selling up the carrier's business and of George being left without neither livelihood nor home — for he lodged in a couple of rooms above the waggon-shed at Erskine's yard — must be a constant and gnawing worry; one which threatened the secure future George had planned upon building in Barrowby.

'I do understand your commitments at the yard, George,' commented Keziah ruefully. 'You really had no need accompanying me today, I told you that.'

'Aye,' he muttered, his gaze set dead ahead upon the desolate track winding across the miles to Keepers Ford. 'I'm no fool, Kez, and I wasn't about to let you come out here without me!'

★　★　★

This was the first occasion Keziah had seen the cottage in daylight.

It was a neat little place, with a well-tended flower and herb garden to the frontage, and to the south-westerly side, Keziah spotted the damson, apple and plum trees of a small orchard curving around to the rear of the cottage.

George was tying the waggon to a fence-post at the corner of the small paddock where the grey horse still grazed, eyeing them balefully. An uncomfortable notion came to Keziah that the docile mare must have witnessed whomsoever entered Mr Bell's cottage uninvited, and later watched that person making his escape after striking down the elderly gentleman.

Keziah slowly approached the low front door, and couldn't help but envisage the cottage as it had been upon the night she'd arrived with Benedict, consumed with anticipation and desperate hopes of recovering Gran's book ... little guessing what awaited them within the unlit rooms.

Preoccupied with her thoughts, Keziah hardly noticed the murmuring of men's voices, somewhere nearby but out of sight beyond the cottage. Stepping up to the front door, she reached out, hesitating before firmly grasping the bell-pull and gently ringing.

The slightly crooked front door was snatched open almost at once by a thin-faced, dour little woman wearing a neat apron and cap, whom Keziah assumed to be Mrs Wickes, the daily woman who had walked up from the neighbouring village each day to cook and clean for Joshua Bell.

'You're expected,' said Edna Wickes bluntly, glancing over her shoulder as, from a rear door directly opposite down the passage, Augustus Bell, Reverend Kennard and Benedict Clay entered from the garden, still engaged in pleasant conversation.

' — Ah, good afternoon, Miss Sephton,' greeted Bell amiably, spying his guests and at once starting along the shadowy passageway. 'Good afternoon to you — '

Keziah met his welcoming smile, moving across the threshold. 'Good — '

'Careful, Kez!' warned George, lunging forward and grasping her arm. 'Watch your step there — There's a big drop!'

'*Oh!*'

Faltering, Keziah quickly turned and glanced up at him, but George wasn't looking at her. He was glaring contemptuously at the three gentlemen standing before them, his stony expression plain even in the poor light of the passageway.

'Good gracious, Miss Sephton! I do beg your pardon!' exclaimed Augustus Bell apologetically, hurrying forward. 'It was most remiss of me not to have had the foresight to ensure a lamp be lit within the sconce there! Even in daytime, this passageway is dark and the step cannot be seen — I frequently warned Joshua one day there would be an accident! I trust you are not hurt?'

'No, not at all!' she insisted, flustering slightly as Mrs Wickes banged the front door closed and took firm hold of Keziah's thick coat, whipping it from her and away to the hall stand.

'When we arrived, I couldn't help noticing,' went on Keziah absently, striving to converse calmly despite the sudden trammels of her thoughts, 'there — there are some fine fruit trees in the orchard . . . Mostly damson and apple, I think?'

'Indeed, indeed,' sighed Augustus with a small smile, ushering them past the ajar door of the study. 'My brother was an enthusiastic gardener, Miss Sephton! The little orchard was Joshua's particular pride and joy. Mr Kennard is also a keen horticulturist, and I've been showing him and Mr Clay the gardens and Joshua's efforts to grow certain fruits under glass, as one frequently sees upon much larger scale in the great houses.'

Keziah realised Augustus was still discussing the garden, but she didn't absorb a single word.

Her attention was riveted upon the

study. She glimpsed only a fleeting view as the party passed by towards the larger room beyond, but it was sufficient for Keziah to see the study was restored to the order and neatness which had doubtless been its custom during Joshua Bell's lifetime. She saw again his old gold pocket watch, still hanging at the chimney-piece, ticking away time. Nothing was out of place. All was as exactly as it should be, yet as Augustus Bell led them into a tastefully furnished room overlooking the orchard, Keziah could not rid her imagination of the memory of Joshua Bell's book-lined study as was upon that dreadful evening she and Benedict entered his cottage.

Keziah sipped her tea, allowing others to make polite conversation. Her gaze fixed upon a framed likeness of Joshua and Mrs Bell, captured for the occasion of their wedding, perhaps. They'd been a handsome couple. She stared at their joyful faces, forcing herself to swallow the hot, fragrant tea. Keziah found she was having increasing difficulty breathing normally. There was a hollow ache in the pit of her stomach and her heart was pounding as she strove to gain control of her spiralling senses; to quell this horrifying panic gripping her mind and heart.

She became aware of Benedict's studying her from beneath lowered lids. Her hands were trembling. Benedict saw, and Keziah squirmed beneath his scrutiny. Summoning the courage to raise her eyes and meet his appraising gaze, she believed somehow Benedict realised the torment raging deep within her, whilst nobody else was even noticing her distress. His dark gaze held her own unflinchingly, yet Keziah could not begin to fathom the enigmatic expression she witnessed in the depths of Benedict Clay's sombre eyes.

She willed the social niceties to be swiftly over, however it was not until afternoon tea was duly served and Mrs Wickes had withdrawn, that Augustus Bell rose from his seat. Crossing the room, the elderly clergyman withdrew a small package from an elegant walnut cabinet.

'Upon the very day Mr Clay brought me news of Joshua's death, I received this package.'

It was carefully wrapped in thick brown paper, tied with string and freshly re-sealed. Augustus offered it to Keziah.

'I have a great interest in old books, you see, Miss Sephton. Especially those of a sacred nature. My brother always looked out for any books I might add to my little collection.

'Joshua's posting the Book of Hours to me was one of the last things he did in this life,' concluded Augustus softly. 'Mr Clay has explained the — confusion — concerning the book's being sold away from your family. I would deem it a great favour if you will allow me to return it to your safekeeping.'

Keziah raised incredulous eyes from Meggan's precious book, and shook her head.

'I — I couldn't accept it, sir!' she stammered at last, deeply moved by Augustus Bell's selfless gesture. 'Thank you humbly, but your brother intended this book for *you!* It's right and proper you keep it. It's what Mr Bell wanted — but thank you so much for your kindness!'

'Miss Sephton, to Joshua and me, this is a book,' began the clergyman gently, a rueful smile touching his lips. 'An old and beautiful sacred book to be sure, but merely a book. It would sit amongst my collection of many other such books. To your grandmother and to your family, however, this little book is treasure beyond price.

'Take the Book of Hours home to your grandmother, Miss Sephton,' Augustus Bell persisted quietly. 'Where it truly belongs . . . '

★   ★   ★

It was but a short while before Keziah and George took their leave.

The cottage door had barely closed behind them when she heard George sigh expansively. He'd been grim-faced and taciturn throughout the afternoon, however when Keziah looked at him now, there was a peculiar mirth spreading across his face.

'That was a turn-up!' he muttered, striding ahead towards the waggon. 'Who'd have thought — '

'I have to go back inside!' blurted Keziah, freezing where she stood, her back ramrod-straight.

'Why?' George queried carelessly, unhitching the reins from the fence-post and adding dryly, 'Haven't left the book behind, have you?'

'No!' she cried, hastily turning on her heel. 'I — I've forgotten my gloves — '

George wasn't paying any attention. He was already bringing around the waggon towards the gate, impatient to be away from Keepers Ford.

'Quick as you can, then!' he called over his shoulder. 'I've a job to get back to and Erskine'll be having my guts for boot-straps — Not as that'll matter much longer, mind!'

Keziah had already rung the bell and was entering Joshua Bell's cottage for the third time, almost colliding with Benedict Clay in the passageway.

'I'm glad you came back,' he murmured urgently, clasping both her shoulders and searching her anguished eyes. 'I was about to come after you . . . '

It was mere minutes before Keziah emerged from the cottage once again and, composed now, walked briskly to the waggon. She accepted George's hand and clambered up onto the seat beside him. When they drove away, she didn't look back.

They'd scarcely cleared the cottage gates and turned onto the track before George gave a long, low whistle.

'I can hardly believe it, Kez!' he whooped euphorically, turning to her in amazement. 'You've got the book back! After all the fuss and bother about scraping together the brass to buy it off Bell, and then finding out it was gone and figuring it was lost forever, *you've got it back!*

'Got it back, lass!' repeated George triumphantly. 'And it hasn't cost a penny-piece in the getting!'

'It may have cost Joshua Bell his life!' snapped Keziah coldly, avoiding looking at George as she gently smoothed her gloved hands across the brown-paper package on her lap. 'None of us — least of all Granny — would wish to have the book at such a price.'

'Don't talk daft! That book means everything to Meggan! If you take my advice, you won't spoil it for her by telling her about Bell buying it as a present for his brother, either,' reasoned George practically. 'Why make her miserable about summat she doesn't need to know?'

They'd driven on a mile or so more before Keziah happened to glance about her and caught sight of the lone rider some considerable distance behind.

Benedict Clay's silhouette was distinctive to her against the pale sky, with its low cloud and deepening shades of sundown. He slowly raised an arm in acknowledgement and Keziah resisted the impulse to respond, thinking wiser of alerting George to Benedict's presence. At first, she wondered whether the American would catch them up and accompany the waggon back to Barrowby. It soon became obvious, however, this was not his intention. Benedict remained at a distance. Nonetheless, Keziah was immensely reassured by his being there.

' . . . Least said, soonest mended; that's best, Kez. Whoever killed Bell is probably a tinker or vagrant. Long gone and never to be seen around these parts again,' George was saying, and Keziah tentatively half-turned to assess her companion.

His stolid features were unusually flushed and animated, his eyes narrowed shrewdly, locked upon the bleak road ahead but plainly seeing a far more agreeable prospect unfolding before him.

' . . . It's been a bad do for you, Kez,' he was expounding. 'It's all over now though. You've got the book back, and it looks like Samuel's finally learned his lesson! He's towing the line in the apothecary, and I've not seen him racketting round town with the Baldwins and Reggie Crane lately either.'

'Sammy's settled to his responsibilities,' she commented, her throat dry and tight. 'Pa and Gran always said he would, and they were right.'

'I don't recall that pair ever being wrong about folk!' grinned George, geeing the horse as they traversed the muddy waters of the ford. 'What with the fever at Quarry End dying down so your pa's not going there as much, Sam pulling his weight and young Betsy learning the ropes in the shop, happen it's high time you and me started making plans, Kez!

'Like as not, Sam and Betsy will get wed, and after she moves into the apothecary, there'll be no need for you to stay there keeping house and looking after your gran and Edith, will there? What I'm saying is — '

'I really don't want to talk today,' she cut in sharply, almost certain what George had been about to propose and not wishing to hear it. They'd never spoken outright about marriage — and now it was all too late.

Keziah drew in a deep breath of the chill air, wondering if somewhere in the fading light of day, Benedict Clay was still riding behind them, keeping the waggon's steady progress in his sights. 'I'd just like to get home, George,' she whispered. 'Please.'

They spoke no more.

Pinpricks of dull light glimmering through the grey dusk from the windows of Barrowby presently slid into Keziah's view, the rough, rutted dirt track of open country was left behind and the waggon's wheels rattled over the cobbles of the town, winding through the shadowy streets and across the market square towards Elijah and Samuel Sephton's apothecary. Samuel was showing out a customer, hailing Keziah and George from the shop's doorway as the waggon slowed to a halt.

Bidding George a hasty goodbye, Keziah scrambled down to the street, the Book of Hours clutched tight against her breast.

'I'd best get straight off,' muttered George distractedly, his thoughts occupied with other concerns. 'And I've a load of timber to pick up first thing, so I'll not be taking you to the bank like usual . . . '

He drove off, turning from the square in the direction of Erskine's yard.

Relieved to be home, Keziah stood alone a moment, drawing her breath before putting a hand to the apothecary's door. Pausing on the threshold, she searched the gathering darkness, her heart lurching at the sight of a lone horseman riding unhurried from the shadows towards her.

Keziah waited, so she and Benedict might enter the apothecary together.

'Are you alright?' he murmured close to her ear, as Edith excitedly ran through the shop to greet them. 'You and I have arrangements to make, Keziah, but first . . . your grandmother's book!'

She nodded, gazing up into Benedict's dark eyes and drawing strength and courage from everything she saw there. Tomorrow, she would have to face George, and do what she must. But tonight . . . Tonight she needed to concentrate her every thought upon her family and upon Benedict Clay.

Tomorrow, with its terrible and inevitable consequences, would come soon enough.

★ ★ ★

Benedict and Keziah were alone together in the kitchen, talking quietly while the rest of the family celebrated the return of the Book of Hours.

' . . . I wish I could stay with you this evening,' he said ruefully, when their discussions were concluded. 'I must pay a call on Constable Towler before I leave town — '

'You're leaving?' She spun around in alarm, the tea kettle in her hands. 'Where are you going?'

'After you left Mr Bell's cottage the second time this afternoon,' he explained calmly, 'the reverends and I talked things through a good deal. We've arranged to meet again tonight at Keepers Ford and plan the wisest course of action.

'What none of us can afford,' Benedict concluded, reaching for his hat and topcoat, 'is to make any careless mistakes. Everything must run like clockwork, if we're to be successful.'

'I'm afraid,' mumbled Keziah, gazing up at him with her heart in her eyes. 'After everything that's happened . . . It's *dangerous*, Benedict!'

'I know, Kezzie, I know,' he murmured, drawing her into his arms for the very first time and holding her close against him, stroking the softness of her hair. 'I'll come by early in the morning and tell you what's been decided.'

'*Benedict!*' she breathed his name, raising her face to his.

Their kiss was urgent and yearning, leaving Keziah aching and bereft when finally, reluctantly, they parted.

'Until tomorrow, my dearest!' was all Benedict said, and then was gone.

★ ★ ★

The following morning, the clock of St Harmon's was chiming the quarter and Keziah was on her knees in the Baldwin family pew, dusting and polishing the ornately carved oak settles before arranging into place the old and richly embroidered kneelers she and Meggan had spent a good many hours repairing and restoring.

She was fraught, her breathing quick and shallow while she worked and waited. At the creak of the west door's opening wide on its ancient hinges, Keziah jolted back on her heels, her head snapping around to see George carrying in a bound tea-chest, depositing it unceremoniously into the corner behind the font.

'What are you doing here?' he exclaimed, straightening up and striding up the nave towards her. 'Oh! I should've guessed — fussing on comforts for the Baldwins! Why can't they kneel on the bare floor like ordinary folk? And why should you be at their beck and call?'

'I really don't mind,' replied Keziah hastily, scrambling to her feet and clutching the kneeler she held with both hands. 'It was only some sewing. Gran and I did it together. Reverend Kennard asked us — '

'I might've have known!' George sneered, shoving his hands into his pockets. 'Kennard's a fine one for pulling strings and roping folk in to do his bidding!

'You do realise I should be on my way to Mounsdale to deliver that timber I was telling you about?' he went on irritably. 'But this morning Erskine says the timber can wait and orders me to get down to the canal and pick up three tea-chests for the church — Course Erskine and Kennard are thick as thieves, so whatever the vicar wants, muggins here has to jump to and be quick about it!'

Keziah was standing with barely a yard's distance separating her from George. Standing and listening. Saying nothing. Hearing him grumbling about ordinary affairs as though this were an ordinary day like any other, and the only thing out of sorts was a tiresome errand for the vicar. Suddenly, Keziah could bear the pretence and the deception no longer.

'Why did you go to Keepers Ford that day?' she demanded, her voice and body trembling uncontrollably. 'You were supposed to be driving to Hawbeck for Mr Erskine! Why did you go to the cottage instead?'

'What's all this about, Kez?' he asked warily. 'I didn't go to the cottage. I went to Hawbeck. I'd never even been to

Keepers Ford 'til we went there yesterday afternoon!'

'That's not true,' Keziah heard herself say, feeling queerly detached as though this were happening to someone else and not to her. 'You'd been to Keepers Ford before, George,' she persisted evenly. 'You'd been *inside* Mr Bell's cottage before!'

'Don't talk daft!' he blustered, his snort of laughter loud and incongruous. 'I'm telling you, I'd not been to that cottage till yesterday!'

'Then how did you know about the steep step behind the front door?' she challenged, her grey eyes sparkling. 'It can't be seen from the threshold!'

Uttering an oath, George turned away from her.

'I don't expect you to understand,' he began at length, dropping heavily into one of the pews, elbows propped on his knees and his bowed head in his hands. 'I had sight of a fortune, Kez — That's summat *no man* can walk away from!'

'The priory silver!' groaned Keziah

miserably, her arms wrapped tight about her. Her quiet words were reverberating up around the high vaulted ceiling, echoing eerily and crowding back into her ears. 'It's naught but a fanciful old story! A child's fairytale about treasure — There's no fortune hidden in Monks Quay!'

'Isn't there?' he challenged angrily, getting to his feet and pacing, his restive footsteps rasping and ringing out upon the worn stone flags. 'Could be there's far more than silver, too! Even *I've* heard tell how rich them holy houses were, and about the gold bowls and cups and jewelled crosses they had in their churches!

'Granted, when we used to be in your house talking about the treasure with Edith and your gran, I may have taken the old story with a pinch of salt, but I still reckoned one day it'd be well worth going to Monks Quay and searching the priory ruins,' argued George vehemently. 'There was no rush. I thought I could go after you'd come of age and got the book and we'd been wed.'

'Then the Book of Hours went missing,' she commented, unable to look at him.

'Aye, and when the lad in the stationer's told us a learned gent like Joshua Bell — a scholar who'd have knowledge of such things — had snapped up the book,' explained George matter-of-factly, 'that was when I knew — *knew for certain* — the tales of hidden treasure were true!'

She shook her bowed head sorrowfully. 'For pity's sake, George — '

'That old man was on the track of the silver, Kez!' he cut in contemptuously. 'He wouldn't have handed over that book — and I wasn't going to stand by and let a fortune slip through my fingers!'

'You took Joshua Bell's life.' She could barely frame the words, but Keziah's eyes met George's without flinching. 'You *murdered* him!'

'I never meant the old man any

harm!' he protested, going on rapidly, 'When I got there, the cottage was deserted. It's a lonely spot, there was nobody to see me, so I got inside and saw that room filled with books. I reckoned your gran's book had to be in there somewhere. I was searching for it when the old man came back and barged into the study . . . '

His voice trailed off. Keziah was no longer looking at him. She was staring past him, beyond him, into the shadowy depths of this ancient sacred place where countless generations of folk had brought their joy and their grief.

'You struck him down.'

'I swear, I didn't raise a hand to that old man!' declared George earnestly. 'He came at me with a damn great staff. Caught me unawares and nearly brained me — I had to defend myself, Kez!'

'You're lying!' She was sobbing now, the horror overwhelming. 'When Benedict and I arrived at the cottage, Mr Bell's ash walking stick was *still* in the

305

hall stand — He *didn't* attack you!'

'Alright, alright,' snapped George desperately. 'Bell got a good look at me so there was no point making a run for it. Only a fool would face transportation or the noose when they could get clean away!

'I had no choice, can you not see that?' he began furiously, breaking off, half-turning away. 'I wanted that fortune, Kez. I want *you*! For us to have a good life together — I wasn't about to let anybody rob me of my chance!'

When he faced Keziah once more, George had regained control of his temper, and there was a slyness coming to his shrewd eyes that made her skin crawl.

'We have the book now, though, don't we?' he wheedled softly. 'So it's not too late . . . We can still have that life together, you and me.'

'How?' she gasped incredulously, her gentle eyes blazing. '*How*? There can be no going back!'

'Kez, I'm no murderer. In your heart of hearts, you know that, don't you? Like I said, I'd no choice but do what I did,' he sighed, and lightly slipping his hands about her waist, George slowly lowered his face closer to hers. 'Nobody knows I was at the cottage that night . . .'

'*I know!*' retorted Keziah, shaking free from the repellent touch of his hands. 'I've known since yesterday afternoon and I *couldn't* keep silent, George — not about murder!'

Steadily, deliberately, he took a step forwards, closing the distance she had created between them.

'Then it shall be your word against mine — '

'*And ours!*'

An imperious, invisible voice rang out within the church walls. Reverend Cyril Kennard slowly emerged from a well of shadows beyond the arched doorway in the north chancel wall. Accompanying him were Augustus Bell and Benedict Clay, with Robert Towler a pace or two from their side.

'We three were witness to your warning Miss Sephton against the step in Joshua Bell's cottage yesterday,' the clergyman continued sombrely. 'And with God as our witness, we, together with Constable Towler, have this day heard your testament, George Cunliffe.'

Reverend Kennard stood aside. 'Do your duty, Mr Towler . . . '

* * *

News that George Cunliffe had been arrested and had admitted his guilt tore through Barrowby, shocking those townsfolk who'd called him friend or neighbour.

George had been more than friend and neighbour to the Sephtons, however. He had been as one of their own. Known to them since he arrived in Barrowby as a penniless boy from the country seeking work, Keziah and her family grieved for what George had done at Keepers Ford, and for the fate that heinous crime had brought him to.

In the weeks that followed, each in their own way struggled to bring order to a confusion of conflicting thoughts and feelings. And yet, in a peculiar way, life for the Sephtons went on as it always had. Every day at the apothecary and in the house had its routine and its chores, and there in the steadfastness of her family and home, Keziah gradually found a measure of stillness to temper the tumble of emotions occupying her heart and mind.

The days of spring were lengthening, and with them came the spring-cleaning and sprucing-up of house and shop. Keziah and Betsy Sharples were busy polishing the small square panes of the bow-fronted windows and door of the apothecary until they shone.

'Only trouble with sunshine,' observed Betsy, standing back to consider her handiwork and giving one pane an extra-vigorous rub. 'It shows up even the tiniest smear left on the glass!'

'True, but we've done a sterling job, Betsy!' declared Keziah, smiling across at the younger woman. Betsy had left domestic service at Castlehill without a backward glance, declining a position selling hats at Barrowby's fashionable little milliner in favour of joining Keziah at the apothecary. 'We've the cleanest windows in the whole of Yorkshire!'

Samuel emerged from the dispensary, carrying a case of freshly-made liniment, and paused alongside the two women, elbowing Betsy and nodding towards one of the sparkling glass panes. 'You've missed a corner!' He grinned. 'You need to take the cloth to it.'

'I'll take a cloth to you in a minute!' she retaliated, feigning to reach into the water-and-vinegar pail for the wet rag. 'On second thoughts, I'd best not. If you drop that liniment, it'll be Keziah and me who'll have to clear up the mess!'

'You're only — ' he began.

'Sammy — Do not say another word!' warned Keziah, gathering up the pails. 'Go back into the dispensary with Pa and behave yourself — There're women hard at work out here!

'I think we deserve a nice pot of tea,' she went on, with a wink to Betsy, after Samuel had obediently made himself scarce. 'The scones should be about ready to come out of the oven now, too. I'll take a tray out to Gran; she's been sitting in the yard crocheting since breakfast was cleared.'

'Aye, a bit of warm sun makes a big difference.' Betsy nodded, taking her place behind the counter and slightly adjusting a display of prettily bottled rose-water. 'Cheers us all up, I reckon. And Mrs Worsley's getting about grand now — I couldn't believe it when I saw her walking in to church last week!'

'Oh, there's no stopping Granny when she sets her mind to something! She was determined to be at St Harmon's and hear the banns for you and Samuel,' beamed Keziah, heading through the arch into the house. 'Gran wouldn't have missed that day for the world, Betsy; none of us would. You and Sammy make a lovely couple, and it's grand you're getting wed!'

Keziah took the tray of tea and oatmeal scones, together with a pat of butter and a dish of last summer's bramble jam, out into the walled yard behind the apothecary.

As a child, she'd helped her mother tend a tiny garden patch out here, and since her passing, Gran and Keziah — and now Edie, too — nurtured the little flowers and plants through the harsh winters, bitter winds and torrential downpours of Barrowby's climate. These recent days of sunshine were coaxing fresh green leaves to uncurl upon the bushes, and glimmering golden-yellow, pale purple and white petals were already peeping from buds soon to burst.

Meggan had set aside her crochet. The seashell shawl of softest wool for

Betsy's wedding day was nearly finished, and Meggan was sitting with her back to the warming sunlight, her face content and her head bowed in concentration as she read the Book of Hours.

That precious family book meant so much to her!

Keziah paused with the tray, standing absolutely still for a moment. How thankful she was Meggan need never know why George went to Joshua Bell's cottage! Nobody ever would be privy to that information, save for those present at St Harmon's upon the morning of the arrest. George's full confession and admission of guilt had spared witnesses the duty of giving evidence against him.

Now, taking a deep breath of crisp spring air, Keziah stepped forward and Meggan glanced up from her reading.

'My, that tray looks a sight for sore eyes!' she exclaimed, closing the pages of the old book. ''Thought I could smell baking!'

'Your favourite brambleberry scones,' smiled Keziah, balancing the laden tray. 'A special treat!'

'You're spoiling me! I've done nowt all morning but crochet and read,' responded Meggan, reaching for her keepsake box and carefully placing the Book of Hours inside. 'It was right kind of Reverend Bell to give this back to us, Kezzie! I'll never be able to thank him enough, for I'd have been letting down your ma if I couldn't pass the book on come your special birthday — It's only a few months off, too!'

'It's a shame Benedict hasn't recognised any of the names written inside, though,' remarked Keziah thoughtfully, setting the tray down across her grandmother's lap. 'Searching for his roots and finding his family means so much to him!'

'The world is a big and lonely place if you've neither kith nor kin to call your own,' agreed Meggan softly, her eyes filled with understanding as she studied her granddaughter's pensive face. 'Benedict's a good man with a good heart, Kezzie, and I have a feeling one day he'll find exactly what he's been seeking!'

'I hope you're right. He'll be leaving Barrowby soon, although we're fortunate he's stayed here as long as he has,' she commented despondently, but added more optimistically, 'At least he still plans upon returning to England in October — and he told me he has something to ask us when he comes for supper.'

'Hmm, I wonder what it might be!' mused Meggan sagely, buttering a feather-light oatmeal scone. 'Which reminds me, I must get a jug of cream from the dairy this afternoon. I'm baking a proper American dessert, Kezzie. One of your grandpa's very own recipes — Applesauce cake, with pouring cream.'

'I've never heard of *that* before, Gran!'

'Well, it *is* a cake, but they have it more like we'd eat a baked pudding,' went on Meggan enthusiastically. 'You see, when my Frank was chef at Rutherfords — that's the finest hotel in Liverpool — there were lots of rich American guests who wanted the kind of food they were used to back home. Applesauce cake was one such. Frank got the gist of what it tasted like, made up his own recipe, and the Americans loved it — So that's what we're having tonight!

'It'll make supper a special occasion, as a thank-you to Benedict,' she concluded, her gaze resting affectionately upon her eldest granddaughter. 'All of us will miss that young man when he goes back to America, Kezzie. He's been a right good friend to this family.'

'I'll fetch the cream from the dairy,' said Keziah briskly, changing the subject and bending to examine the unfurling petals of the primulas growing in the sheltered warmth of the south-facing stone wall.

'You'll do no such thing!' protested

Meggan firmly. 'Now I'm able to get about on my own two pins again, I'm off out to make the most of this grand spring weather!'

* * *

' . . . I can't recall when I've enjoyed a meal more! Thank you for inviting me,' Benedict was saying that evening, when the family were gathered around the table in the best room and all that remained of the famous applesauce cake was a scattering of crumbs in the serving dish. 'I haven't tasted applesauce cake since I was a boy, Mrs Worsley, and this cake tasted even better than I remember! It was really kind of you to take the trouble of making it.'

'It's one of my Frank's special recipes,' replied Meggan proudly. 'I'm very glad you liked it, Benedict. It were nice, baking summat fancy for a change!'

'It were certainly different,' opined Elijah, reaching for the teapot and refilling his cup. 'But it went down a treat, right enough.'

'How goes your work at the almshouse, sir?' enquired Benedict. Although he'd known Elijah Sephton but a short while, even he had noticed the older man was looking much better these days. The deeply etched lines of exhaustion and strain were gradually fading from the apothecary's features now he was no longer devoting every hour the Lord sent tending the sick and the dying at the almshouse. Fears of the pestilence reaching up from the squalor of Quarry End and engulfing the whole of Barrowby had all but receded. 'Is the threat of fever genuinely over?'

'Nobody has fallen sick for a while, so we're praying that's so. Until the next time,' Elijah answered soberly. 'It'll come back, Benedict. It'll always come back, until the men of this prosperous little town start looking beyond making bigger and bigger profits and show a care for folk less fortunate!'

'Aye, that's true enough, Elijah,' agreed Meggan, adding mildly, 'But can we leave politicking aside, just for tonight?'

'Pa's right, though,' put in Samuel quickly, his handsome face unusually grave. 'I've accompanied him to Quarry End and the almshouse upon several occasions now, and I had no idea how truly appalling it is! Of course, I'd heard Pa speaking about it — and you too, Kezzie, for you regularly take provisions down there — but nothing prepared me for what I saw!

'Pa — and the few other men in Barrowby with compassion and foresight — are absolutely correct,' finished Samuel decisively. 'There must be reform in this town, and it *must* come swiftly!'

Keziah was astonished at Samuel's impassioned outburst. She'd no idea her brother had ever visited Quarry End, nor that he was developing a social and political conscience in town affairs. Glancing along the table to her future sister-in-law, however, Keziah realised none of this was news to Betsy. But then, hadn't she always loved Samuel, seen the very best in him, and believed utterly in his ability to accomplish whatever deeds he set his mind upon?

The conversation drifted onto other things. Presently, while Keziah and Betsy, helped by young Edith, were clearing dishes and making a fresh pot of tea, the little party moved nearer the warmth of the crackling fire. Spring nights in Barrowby were still long and cold.

' . . . I'll be leaving aboard the stage for Liverpool, Edith, where I'm boarding a ship sailing for Charleston,' explained Benedict, in answer to the little girl's questions about his plans. 'And, yes, I am very sad to be going away!

'Actually, that's what I wanted to talk to you all about,' he continued tentatively, displaying a rare uncertainty as he studied the faces of those gathered with him around the hearth. 'As you know, in the fall I'm returning to England and visiting Lancashire, where my family originally came from.

'I recall Mrs Worsley saying she'd like to go back to see her old home and visit her brother-in-law at Monks Quay.' Mindful of six pairs of curious eyes watching him intently, Benedict pressed on. 'I was wondering — hoping — you might all join me on the trip to Lancashire? I believe it's possible to travel swiftly and in considerable comfort with certain stagecoaches.' His gaze fleetingly rested upon Keziah, before taking in the remainder of the gathering. 'It would mean a great deal to me if we could make the journey to Monks Quay together.'

'It's a grand idea!' beamed Elijah, the wind taken from his sails at the unexpected invitation but nonetheless delighted for his family. 'I can't leave the apothecary, mind, but the rest of you'd be daft not to go! 'specially you, Meggan — You can't miss out on summat like this.'

'Neither can you, Pa!' chipped in Samuel, reaching across to tenderly take his sweetheart's hand into his own. 'Betsy and I will take care of the apothecary while you're away, won't we?'

'Course, we will!' she declared contentedly. 'We'll be wed by then, Mr Sephton, so you go off and have a grand holiday with the others — You deserve it!'

'Looks like that's settled then — We're bound for Lancashire! And by the way, lass, it's *Elijah* — or even *Pa*, if that sits easy with you,' beamed Elijah again, leaning forward and taking a spill from the mantel to light his pipe. 'D'you know, I've never seen the sea in my whole life!'

'Neither have I!' piped up Edith, her face flushed with firelight and excitement, barely able to keep still as she sat on the little three-legged stool alongside Keziah's chair. 'Granny's told me about it, and what it looks like, but now we're really and truly going to see the sea!

'I can't wait for October to hurry up and come,' she sighed happily, upturning her face to her big sister. 'Can you, Kezzie?'

Keziah couldn't speak, so overwhelmed was she at the tantalising prospect of being reunited with Benedict — of actually travelling with him across country all the way out to the wild and rugged Lancashire coast!

Smiling down at Edith, she ruffled the little girl's tawny hair and murmured some response. The lively conversation around the fireside was already caught up with plans for the trip and Meggan's reminiscences. Keziah was content to sit unobtrusively, saying nothing and scarcely taking heed of a word being said. In the intimacy the shadowy firelight afforded, she had the rare luxury of gazing at Benedict Clay without risk of her attentions being observed.

It was bittersweet pleasure indeed!

For while there was solace in the knowledge she and Benedict would meet again, Keziah ached with sadness and a longing she could not subdue. For in but a few short days, he would be leaving her.

Keziah would smile, bid him a cheerful farewell and wish him God-speed, but her heart would break at the moment of parting from Benedict Clay, and in facing the prospect of their being separated by thousands of miles of land and ocean.

★　★　★

On the Sunday before he was leaving Barrowby, Benedict hired a carriage and drove the Sephtons down to the river, following its winding course away from the town and out into open countryside.

It was a bright and sunny May after-noon and no sooner had Benedict tethered the horses beneath the waterside white willows than Edith scrambled down from the open-topped carriage and was away running through the rough grass towards the water's edge.

'There're ducklings on the river!' she called over her shoulder, beckoning for everybody to follow her. 'Five of them! Come and see!'

'We'll keep an eye on Edith,' offered Betsy, intuitively sensing Keziah's melancholy mood and guessing her friend would want these precious few hours before Benedict's departure alone in his company. '*Won't* we, Samuel?'

'We can take her up to the wishing bridge,' he responded helpfully. 'When she was tiny, Edie loved my taking her to the wishing bridge.'

'That's a good idea!' agreed Elijah enthusiastically, catching the gist of what was going on. 'Isn't it, Meggan? What say you and me sit a spell over yonder to admire the view and then stroll down-river to the Wild Swan?'

'A nice stroll and tea at the Swan will suit me grand!' responded Meggan, settling comfortably in the sunshine.

Gazing across the rushing river and away above the fresh greenery of the woodland to the distant russet hills, she drew a deeply contented breath — Suddenly aware of Keziah and Benedict's patiently hovering on the riverbank, Meggan turned to flap a hand dismissively in their direction.

'Don't let us olduns hold you up! Away the pair of you go and enjoy the day,' she insisted. 'You can collect Elijah and me from the Wild Swan later.'

' . . . your grandmother is remarkably perceptive — and discreet!' murmured Benedict with a wry smile, when he and Keziah were walking, arm in arm, beside the sun-dappled, sparkling river. White willow and alder lined the inland side of the wide grassy bank, while tall feathery reeds and clusters of bright, wavering yellow flag fringed the water's edge. 'I was hoping we'd somehow have time alone together.'

'I can't believe by tomorrow you'll be

gone!' she blurted, her grey eyes huge when she looked up at him. 'I wish you weren't leaving!'

'So do I,' he replied softly. 'You do understand that, don't you?'

She nodded, turning quickly to watch the deep, eddying river so he could not see the treacherous tears that would not be blinked back.

'It's just . . . October's a long way off and Charleston is so very far away, Benedict!'

'*I know!*'

Placing a cool fingertip against Keziah's warm lips, Benedict silenced her words.

'I love you, Keziah — I've probably loved you since that very first day, when I went into the apothecary and you came walking through the archway like someone I've waited my whole life to meet!

'I came to these shores in search of my family's past,' he breathed, taking her into his arms. 'Instead I believe I've found my own future — if only you will agree to sharing it with me . . . '

A little further down the riverbank, Meggan and Elijah were still settled in the warm sunshine, enjoying the fine afternoon.

' . . . it's a right shame Benedict didn't recognise the names in your book,' Elijah was remarking, shielding his eyes and watching the family of ducks grazing the coarse grass. 'I wonder will he find any kinfolk when we go over Lancashire come autumn? Pity he's not related to us, though, for he's a grand lad.'

'Benedict might not be a blood relative,' commented Meggan, nudging Elijah in the ribs to divert his attention from the ducklings and up along the bank to where Benedict and Keziah were lingering in the shelter of the white willows. 'But if I'm any judge, he's set to be one of the family true enough!'

Although neither Meggan nor Elijah could hear a word being spoken by Keziah and Benedict, they observed the tender kiss sealing the couple's joyful promise.

'Aye, happen you're right there, Meggan,' agreed Elijah placidly, drawing contentedly upon his pipe. 'Happen you're right!'

THE END